the party room

LAST CALL

MORGAN BURKE

SIMON PULSE

New York London Toronto Sydney

This book is a work of fiction. Any references to historical events, real people, or real locales are used fictitiously. Other names, characters, places, and incidents are the product of the author's imagination, and any resemblance to actual events or locales or persons, living or dead, is entirely coincidental.

 SIMON PULSE
An imprint of Simon & Schuster Children's Publishing Division
1230 Avenue of the Americas, New York, NY 10020

Copyright © 2005 by Parachute Publishing, L.L.C.
All rights reserved, including the right of reproduction in whole or in part in any form.

SIMON PULSE and colophon are registered trademarks of Simon & Schuster, Inc.

A Parachute Press Book
Designed by Greg Stadnyk
The text of this book was set in Photina.
Manufactured in the United States of America
First Simon Pulse edition June 2005

10 9 8 7 6 5 4 3 2 1

Library of Congress Control Number 2004111862
ISBN 0-689-87227-5

Part One

The Brother

The chirping sound of Outkast's "Hey Ya!", as played by cell phone, interrupted the conversation. Kirsten made a mental note to change that. It was embarrassing. "Hello?" she said, answering the phone.

There was a pause at the other end. And then a voice said, "Kirsten? Is this Kirsten Sawyer?" The voice was muffled and distorted—a hugely bad cell phone connection.

"You have to speak up," Kirsten said. "Who is this?"

"Kirsten," the voice said, "you don't know me. My name is Rich Stone."

Kirsten swallowed hard. Julie, noticing the change in Kirsten's face, dropped her burger and was staring intently across the table.

"S-Stone?" Kirsten repeated, her pulse quickening. "As in—"

"I'm Paul's brother," the voice interrupted. "*Kyle's* brother. I need to talk to you. It's a matter of life and death."

Prologue

It's over.

That's what I've been telling myself.

Completely over. Done. History.

It was a perfect summer. Not a bad fall, either. Peaceful. And now it's February in New York, snow on the ground, chicks in sweaters, meat in the freezer and spices in the cupboard, and I should be in a great mood.

Hey, what's past is past and what's dead is dead. Memories can't hurt you.

So why am I feeling it again? What's wrong with me?

WHY AM I FEELING IT?

Is it because they're back? That must be it. They're back for winter break. Back from three months of taking drugs and screwing each other at Harvard and Yale and Princeton and Brown, where they never would have been accepted but for Mom and Dad's seven-figure donations. Yes, that must be it. They're back, and their smug faces are reminding me of the . . . the . . .

Incidents.

Preppy Murders. That's what they called

them. Well, guess what, they're not MURDERS if they happen for a reason.

Carolee . . . Sam . . . Emma . . . I had to kill them.

DAMN IT, THEY HAD TO GO! Sometimes justice requires sacrifice. And the sacrifice has been made. Three times. More than enough, thank you very much.

No, not enough. One more. The prize—Kyle—the one who liked to pretend he was so innocent. I enjoyed putting him down most of all.

BUT IT WAS SUPPOSED TO BE OVER AFTER THAT—NO MORE!

So why do they ruin it? Why do they bring it all back? They remind me. They taunt me . . . HELLO? WAKE UP, PAL. WHAT ARE YOU TALKING ABOUT? THOSE KIDS ARE MEAN-INGLESS. I shouldn't give a shit about the ones who are here. The ones who remind me . . . . I got RID of the bad ones—the ones who made trouble.

It's something else. Something else is getting me juiced. So what is it?

I know.

It's the cops. I'm seeing too many cops.

Are they after me? How can they know? THERE'S NO ONE LEFT TO TELL THEM A GODDAMN THING. Except . . .

Except . . . for her. For Kirsten.

She'd better not be stirring up bad feelings again. She should let it rest if she knows what's good for her. . . .

No, she knows. She knows what will happen. Taught by example.

No, it's paranoia. It's got to be.

Paranoia is the enemy, pal. Paranoia means lack of control. And it's all about control. CONTROL is my middle name.

So I'll nose around a little if I have to. Just enough to be sure it's all okay.

And keep a lid on.

Calm down.

Remember, it ain't over till it's over.

And it's over.

Isn't it?

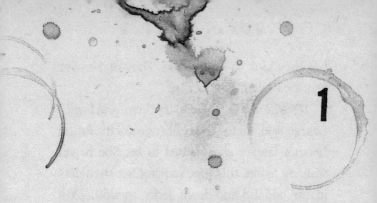

"Shake it a little,"

Kirsten Sawyer said, smiling at the way her new college roommate was teetering on Kirsten's fabulous stiletto-heeled footwear.

"Shake it?" Lauren Chaplin said, pausing on the sidewalk outside their dorm. She turned uncertainly, her pool of ink black hair falling like a shadow across her alabaster forehead. She looked like a small child about to enter kindergarten for the first time. "I have scoliosis. You know, curvature of the spine. It's kind of hard to shake."

"It'll make it easier to walk on those shoes," Kirsten replied.

Lauren sighed. "Does everyone in New York wear Manilas?"

"Manolos," Kirsten corrected her. "You don't have to wear them if you don't want, but they look so hot on you. They make your legs look killer."

"Okay, I *said* I wanted to try them, and I *will*," Lauren said, taking the challenge like the future hotshot lawyer she wanted to be. She began walking again, this time moving her shoulders in an odd up-and-down jerky motion, as if testing some new form of personal outpatient electroshock treatment. "Is this right?"

"Um, better . . . ," Kirsten said as encouragingly as she could. *She'll get it*, she told herself. *Give her an A for effort.*

She liked Lauren. Compared with Kirsten's New York friends, Lauren seemed from another planet—innocent, eager, hardworking, fashion-clueless—and totally refreshing. Totally able to laugh at herself. She was definitely taking the edge off Kirsten's dreaded return to the land of reality.

Arriving in Manhattan in the dead of winter was tough enough for any normal person, but it was a thousand times worse when you'd spent the last few months on a sunny Greek island with nothing but a stack of books, an iPod, some cold drinks, and miles and miles of clothing-optional beaches. Return from that qualified as Severe Reentry Trauma.

Kirsten had only met Lauren, like, five hours ago—in line at registration, along with the few other odd freshmen who had deferred starting college until second semester. To feel good about her first day, Kirsten had dressed in what seemed like the perfect outfit for an NYU freshman—Coach tote, Marc Jacobs pants and sailor coat—nothing too flashy, just a little visual cue that said, "I'm a native New Yorker." But something felt weird. All around the room she could feel people staring at her. Was it her island-bronzed skin, the fiery red sun streaks through her chestnut brown hair . . . outfit envy? Or was it something worse? Did they recognize her? That couldn't be true. They couldn't know who she was. As her good mood began to slip fast, it took all her strength to not bolt for the nearest travel agency—when a voice behind her piped up, "Hey, that's a neat outfit."

It was the phraseology that did it.

"Neat?" Kirsten replied, as if testing a new word in a particularly tricky ancient dialect.

During her entire life on the Upper East Side of Manhattan, right up through four years of the exclusive Woodley School, where hot fashions and cool lingo changed by the week, Kirsten had never, ever heard the word *neat* in the same sentence as *outfit*. She turned to see Lauren's face, smiling and nonjudgmental, framed in the hood of an L.L. Bean anorak. They got to talking, and within minutes Kirsten knew that Lauren had grown up on a farm in Wisconsin, started NYU late because she'd been working with a local environmental law firm on a project that went till January, and was determined to (a) score the grades to go to Yale Law School; (b) find her first boyfriend, and (c) learn how to dress like those girls on *Sex and the City*—in that order. Which wasn't exactly the most auspicious beginning of a friendship, until Kirsten opened her mouth to describe her own personal history—and Lauren hung on every mundane detail as if she were in the presence of a master storyteller. She was a great listener, laughing and friendly, sweet and cheery. The cheeriness was key, since Kirsten had felt an acute cheer deficit in her life.

Lauren had been assigned as her roommate, part of a three-girl suite in a temporary dorm called the Better Ridgefield Hotel—

which, to Kirsten, was totally cool. And they made a pact: Lauren would tell Kirsten about what life is like on a farm, and Kirsten would show Lauren how to dress like a New Yorker.

Which was why Lauren was, at the moment, struggling up the steps of the Better Ridgefield in Kirsten's sexiest pair of Manolo heels, hanging on to the metal banister for dear life. The grungy green backpack that was hanging from her shoulders was way wrong, accessory-wise, but one thing at a time. "I'm getting . . . the hang . . . of it," she said through a brave grimace.

"Just pretend it's easy," Kirsten said, opening the front door.

They walked slowly toward the first-floor lounge, down a musty hallway that smelled of fresh paint and cheap carpet. There was nothing "Better" about the Better Ridgefield, as far as Kirsten could tell. Until this year it had been an abandoned hotel, but the school had bought it for temporary housing while a new dorm was being completed. They had renovated it fast and cheap, and it looked it.

The lounge was a converted old apartment with the walls knocked out, decorated with

5

thrift-store sofas surrounding an old TV. Kirsten's eyes went directly to a hunky blond god on the sofa. Part of her wanted to wink at Lauren—"watch this"—and seduce the guy in seconds flat, but that wasn't really her style. So she sat casually on a thick, padded armchair and smiled hopefully. She did *not* expect Adonis to do a sitcom double take at the sight of Lauren carefully placing one fabulously clad foot in front of the other—or to leap up from his six-foot slouch like a giant cocker spaniel and offer her the spot next to him. "I'm Brad," he said with a smile that could have wiped anyone's slate clean.

Lauren sat, blushing, in the romantic light of a flickering car commercial.

Go, girl, Kirsten thought with a sigh. *Ah, the transforming power of six-inch heels.*

Just like that, Brad had his arm around Lauren, and Kirsten tried to keep her eyes on the TV while some other guy, sitting in an armchair, smiled at her. "You're from the city, aren't you?" he said. He had short brown hair and freckles, and he was built like a linebacker.

"How'd you know?" Kirsten replied.

"I can always tell," he said, which might

have been a harmless observation but sounded vaguely like an insult and made Kirsten wonder what the *hell* it meant. "What's your name?" he continued.

Before Kirsten could react a thin guy wearing an orange knit hat rose from an armchair. His face was angular and rugged, with high cheekbones and a firm jaw. He looked kind of familiar, but Kirsten couldn't figure out why. If he put on a few pounds, maybe rearranged the features a bit, he'd actually be kind of handsome—like that 1950s star with gorgeous hollow eyes, whose perfect face was put back together after a car accident and always looked slightly *off,* slightly ravaged . . . what was his name? Mom had rented some of his movies in Greece. *The Young Lions. The Misfits.* Cliff something. Montgomery Clift. That was it.

"Shhhhhhh!" he called out, his eyes glued to the television. "Yo, people. It's starting! Watch this! *Watch this!*"

The linebacker-guy smiled. "Film geek," he remarked. "Tisch School."

But Kirsten wasn't listening, because the screen was filling up with images of a TV movie, and an earnest voice intoned, "*Next on*

7

this station . . . ripped from today's headlines . . . murder and privilege in the Big City . . . it's a lethal combination. . . ."

There it was, on the TV screen, the Party Room. Her favorite hangout of all time, only more crowded, more crazed than it ever really was—and there, at the bar, tossing her head back with a loud, sexy laugh, was her best friend, Samantha Byrne. Only it wasn't Sam, not really, it was an actress playing Sam, and next to her were two other actresses, both trash-talking and juiced to the gills: one a dead-ringer for Julie Pembroke; and the other—*oh, God*—the other looked just like Kirsten, and she felt herself doubling over, as if hit in the stomach, because this trailer *"ripped from the headlines"* was advertising a TV movie *based on Sam's murder!*

But it was different, weird and exaggerated, as if lifted from a bleak, distorted place in her own mind, the place that held the recurring nightmare she'd had for months, the scenes racing by in quick jump cuts: Sam arguing with her ex-boyfriend, Brandon Yardley . . . Sam walking out of the Party Room arm in arm with Jones, the red-haired drug dealer—the man Kirsten still believed was her murderer . . . a moonlit night in Central Park, Sam with bare shoulders lying in the grass, smiling dreamily into a guy's face . . . not Jones, but another actor— another way-too-familiar face—and then a pair of hands grabbing her wrists and tying them with a blue-and-gold-striped Talcott school tie . . . grabbing a large rock and bludgeoning her head over and over and over. . . .

Kirsten felt a shock that seemed to fry her nerve endings, her brain suddenly numb but her body moving as if it had a life of its own . . . toward the door, away from the TV, away from the memory she'd hoped to put behind her, now flooding her mind like an open wound. And she was vaguely aware of a voice, the guy with the orange hat, hooting with derision at the trailer, calling it cheesy—but *cheesy* wasn't the word Kirsten would have chosen for something like this, something that seemed to mock and stab at the same time.

As she exited the building, the February cold hit her hard.

"Kirsten?" Lauren's voice called from behind her. "Kirsten? *Ow!*"

9

Kirsten turned.

Lauren stood in the doorway, her backpack slung over her shoulders, pulling off the Manolos. "These things are killing me. Wait up. What happened? Why did you leave like that?"

"I had to go . . . to the bathroom," Kirsten said absently as they crossed the street.

"You're lying."

"How do you know?"

"Because you passed the bathroom and we're now outside in the middle of the street in February without any coats—and I'm barefoot." Lauren paused. "It was the movie, wasn't it?"

As they turned onto MacDougal Street, passing small groups of briskly walking students, Kirsten tried to summon an answer. But what could she say? Lauren was so innocent. She had no idea. How do you explain murder and grief to someone who couldn't possibly understand? Lauren was supposed to be part of Kirsten's *new* life—a world away from the murders.

"Kirsten," Lauren said softly. "I know. I know who you are."

Kirsten stopped in her tracks. They were

near the corner of Washington Square Park south and MacDougal, and a light snow was beginning to dust the dog run just inside the park. "You do?"

"They have newspapers in Sheboygan, you know," Lauren replied with a sarcastic lilt. "TVs, too," she added. "I recognized your name from the moment I got the roommate assignment. But don't worry: I won't say a thing if you don't want me to. And we don't have to talk about it—ever."

No, Kirsten thought. She had to talk about it. She had to get it out in the open or else it would be hanging between them for the rest of the year. She exhaled a cumulus puff into the air. When she spoke, the words seemed to come from far away. "The movie has it all wrong, I'm sure," she said. "We weren't that drunk. And Sam . . . she didn't let herself get that out of control. Never. She was wild, but not stupid. Well, not until that night, anyway. She left the bar . . . with a guy named Jones— a drug dealer—she was . . . *involved* with him somehow. . . . He killed her in Central Park . . . at least, I think he did. I don't know for sure. The killer, whoever he was, had killed another

11

girl two years earlier, Carolee Adams, in the same, exact way: beaten and stabbed with a Talcott school tie bound around her wrists. Then he came back and killed again. First Sam, then another girl, Emma, who idolized Sam; tried to be just like her. . . ."

"Why them?" Lauren asked. "Why Sam?"

Kirsten shook her head. "All I know is, Kyle had said he had it all figured out. But that was right before . . ."

"Wait. Kyle?" Lauren spoke up. "Who's he?"

Kirsten sank onto a park bench. How could she explain who Kyle was? Their relationship was so complicated. "I met Kyle at the Party Room one night—and before I knew it, I was in love with him," she told her. "He said he went to Bowdoin College and was in New York visiting a friend. At least that's what he told me, but it wasn't true. His name was really Paul Stone. I'll always know him as Kyle, though."

"Oh, wow," Lauren whispered. "I know that name too. From the papers. But isn't *he* the one the police said committed those murders? And if Kyle and Paul are the same guy . . ." She wrinkled her nose. "But then you said the other guy did it. What was his name? Jones?"

"Kyle was not the killer! That's what everyone thinks, because his Talcott tie was found on Carolee, but he didn't do it. I know it. He was framed. He'd left that tie in some bar. Someone must have taken it—and when it was traced to Kyle, the papers were all over him, printing these ugly mug shots and calling him names. He was convicted in an unfair trial—and he was eventually let go on a technicality. But by then he and his family were ruined. That's why they came to New York—to find the real killer and to clear their family's name," she said. "So maybe the killer got scared. He knew Kyle was on his tail. The only way to get rid of him was to kill again— to murder someone the same way that Carolee was killed. Of course, the world knew Paul Stone was free from jail. The minute someone recognized him, Paul/Kyle would be arrested—this time, they'd throw away the key. So that was the reason for the murders. *That's* why the killer went after . . ." Kirsten couldn't finish the sentence. Her numbness was giving way to tears.

"It's okay, you don't have to talk about it

anymore," Lauren said gently, her voice comforting and reassuring.

"Kyle . . . knew he was in a race," Kirsten said haltingly. "He had to get the killer while he had the chance, before anybody realized who he was. He had lost weight, changed his look—but he wasn't going to fool everyone forever. The thing is, he told me he knew what really went down, Lauren. I think he knew who the killer was—but now we'll never find out!"

"I know, I know," Lauren said, nodding sympathetically. "The pressure must have been so great. Suicide is such a senseless thing—"

"*It wasn't suicide. He was murdered, Lauren!* Don't you see? It's the perfect crime: Frame someone who's already been in jail—someone the public hates—and if he has the guts to try to figure out your identity, kill him and make it look like suicide. Who's going to investigate any further? Case closed."

Lauren was silent for a long time. "So . . . you think the killer's still out there? This Jones guy?"

"That's the only bright spot in the whole story," Kirsten said. "He's in jail—not for murder, though. For dealing drugs."

"You're very brave," Lauren said.

Kirsten smiled. "Yeah, right. That's why I ran away to Greece—and I'd still be there if my mom hadn't gotten tired of feta cheese, olives, and men who spit when they talk."

"Someday, after I graduate Yale Law and I've set up a litigation practice involving the fair and equitable representation of women and minorities, I will represent you in your case against this guy—pro bono. And we'll put him behind bars forever."

"I may take you up on that," Kirsten said. "Even though I barely know you—"

Lauren grinned warmly. "If you want to know me, take me shopping. You were the one who said shopping is a way to discover a person's deepest soul, right?"

"You're learning, girlfriend," Kirsten said with a sly laugh, slowly feeling her sense of humor return. She couldn't let herself dwell on the murders any longer. The whole thing had almost driven her crazy! No, she had to let it go—let go of the guilt—let the police handle whatever investigation was left. It had taken months in therapy to get to this point, but she could finally say that she was at peace with herself now.

Lauren slipped on the Manolos again and stood. "I'm freezing and stressed from this conversation and I desperately need some spearmint chai with lemon to calm my nerves. And so do you. Come on." She yanked Kirsten up and gamely walked with her, a little less wobbly than before, to the student union building.

Kirsten felt spent and sad and torn apart, but the cold was beginning to seep in now, and she really did need something to drink. Something stronger than tea, though. Visions of "Scotty the Hottie's Hot Rum Toddies" danced in her head—a killer winter drink patented at the Party Room by Scott, the hunkiest bartender in town.

That's what she needed. And she'd ask for one tonight. This evening Julie was coming over from Barnard to meet her, and together they planned a night of barhopping like old times. Just the thought of it cheered her up.

The student union's lobby had a huge, vaulted atrium, ringed with balconies that seemed to go up forever. On one side of the main floor were filigreed metal tables with comfy-looking chairs, spilling out from a grill/refreshment area.

Lauren dumped her backpack on the table, pulling out a sheaf of papers. "We can coordinate our schedules and maybe collect some data about our instructors before we choose classes, okay?"

Kirsten glanced at the pile. On top was the revised roommate assignment list they'd received that morning. One of the names had changed.

Jan deVries.
Kirsten Sawyer. Lauren Chaplin. ~~Clarice Moravec~~.

That was weird. Kirsten knew the name Clarice Moravec. Vaguely. From the TV news—the sports part, during which she usually bolted for the fridge. "Isn't Clarice an athlete?" Kirsten asked. "Like, basketball or baseball or something?"

"Basketball," Lauren replied. "A point-per-game average of 29.3 and double digits in both assists and rebounds. How disappointing. She would have been an asset to the suite. Let's just hope Jan is as nice as we are. I'll get the tea."

As Lauren scooted over to the counter with tiny, clackety footsteps on the tile floor, Kirsten stretched, arching her neck back and gazing up at the levels of the circular atrium. *This semester with Lauren is definitely going to be interesting,* she thought.

That's when she saw something plummet down the center of the atrium. She thought at first that someone had dropped a laundry basket.

But laundry didn't have arms and legs.

Laundry didn't scream.

"Oh . . . my . . . GOD!" Kirsten murmured, instinctively leaping up from the table at the same moment that the falling clump—*not a clump, a GIRL, a HUMAN BEING*—hit the floor tiles with a sickening noise like a sack of giant cantaloupes, and then bounced—actually *bounced*—which was the most shocking and sickening thing of all. Kirsten felt every meal she'd had over the last two days fighting to rise up through her chest as screams pierced the air, as people began rushing back and forth, surrounding the body, the lifeless remains of someone alive a moment ago—and a sudden howl rose up around her so loud and jarring that Kirsten didn't even realize it was her own.

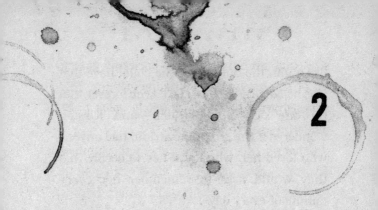

2

Limp.

Broken.

Motionless.

A doll tossed out of a crib.

Dead.

The thoughts ripped into Kirsten's brain in a nanosecond, but it seemed as if time had stopped, and the image before her was morphing . . . her brain trying to match it to another image in her memory, as if that would somehow make sense out of the horror . . . the senselessness . . . and now she saw another corpse, the only other real dead person she'd ever seen besides . . .

Kyle.

Splayed out, his eyes open and pleading, his legs twisted at odd angles, his fingers folded around a photo—a photo she immediately took because he seemed to be offering it, like a gift, the only thing she could have that was his, a piece of him she'd keep forever that no one else could touch—and Kirsten wondered if the girl in the atrium had anyone who loved her, who loved her so deeply that they would *need* to remember her every minute of every day. . . .

And she became acutely aware of the power of death, unexpected death, and for a moment she was grateful and relieved to not know this girl, to not have to suffer the unbearable ache of personal loss—and the cold perverseness of that thought was, finally, what got her moving.

She had to get away. Anywhere else. Outside in the cold air. Away from the noise. The reminders. The death.

No more death.

She staggered through the crowd, clutching her backpack, fighting against the streams of students running every which way. The quiet atrium was a chamber of shrieks, sobs, and the hollow guttural sound of kids puking—one girl against a potted plant, a guy by the window. *Where did they all come from? There weren't that many people here a minute ago.*

She tried to run, but the crowd was too thick. Too many obstacles. And now the police were arriving. Clanking heavily through the open glass doors, their guns and cop paraphernalia bouncing on their belts. Forcing the students to step aside.

Lauren. Where was Lauren?

Ignoring the instinct to avert her eyes, she looked back. The body was blocked from view by a clutch of onlookers. On their periphery Kirsten recognized the guy from the lounge, the skinny film geek with the orange knit hat. He was circling the crowd, holding a camera high above everyone's head, his lens aimed downward toward the dead girl, snapping pictures.

Pictures!

A girl was lifeless and crushed on the floor, a girl whose proud parents at that moment imagined she was alive and healthy but were about to get news that would forever rock their world . . . and this pervert was *taking pictures*!

"Kirsten! Oh, my God. Kirsten! Did you see what happened? Someone jumped!"

Lauren was heading for her, shoes in one hand. *That's right, she had gone off to get us tea.*

Before Kirsten could respond, a bewildered-looking guy wandered over from the front door, wrapped in a down coat and scarf. "What happened?" he asked.

Kirsten pointed upward. "A girl fell from that balcony—like the sixth floor or something."

Scattered around all the balconies, students had gathered to gawk. At the place where the girl had jumped, more or less, stood a guy conspicuous with a shining, shaved head—too old to be a student, probably a teaching assistant. Kirsten's eyes drifted past him and scanned the other faces, all unfamiliar, all frozen with shock. But something about the bald guy—his posture, his body language—was different from everyone else. He seemed distracted, looking around for something on the floor, then glancing disinterestedly downward. . . .

And that was when Kirsten got a good look at his face.

He seemed familiar. She knew him. Somehow.

He wasn't unattractive. His eyes seemed dark and powerful, with a piercing coldness she could feel intensely, even at that distance.

And it was in that glance, in that split

second when his eyes rested a little too long on hers, that she realized who he was.

The hair was gone, but the face was the same. If she imagined him the way she'd last seen him—with a shock of flowing red hair, a drugged-out smile—she knew.

She knew, and she was scared out of her mind.

It was Jones.

"LOOK!" Kirsten blurted out. A cop thundered past her, and she grabbed him by the sleeve, pointing upward. "Look! That guy!"

The officer glanced up—but Jones's face was gone. Disappeared behind the balcony wall.

"Didn't you see him?" Kirsten pleaded.

"Who?" the cop and Lauren asked at the same time.

"The bald guy. His name is *Jones!*" Kirsten said. "He was a suspect in Sam Byrne's murder. A drug dealer. He was put in jail, but now he's out. He was on the balcony where the girl fell. He pushed her—I know it. *He's a killer!* Ask Detective Peterson. He was in charge of the case. Do you know Detective Peterson?"

The cop squinted. "Are you sure it was the same balcony? Did you see where he went?"

"NO! I don't know!"

It was useless. They were staring at her as if she were crazy.

Maybe she *was* crazy. Maybe she needed to follow her original instinct to *go.*

She made a break for the door, pushing her way through and feeling again the shock of February's cold against her perspiration-soaked body.

What was Jones doing out of jail? And why did he push that girl? Who was she? All his victims so far had been linked—Sam, Carolee, Emma—all part of Kirsten's Upper East Side crowd. This girl wasn't one of them.

Was this girl involved in a drug deal gone bad? Was that the reason he killed her? She turned up MacDougal, shivering, pulled out her cell phone, and punched Detective Peterson's number.

"KIRSTEN! HEY, WAIT!" Lauren ran up alongside her, her breaths puffing in the frigid air. "Are you okay?"

Kirsten put her fingers to her lips, shushing her friend. On the other end of the phone, Peterson picked up right away. Just like the old days. "Peterson."

"It's Kirsten. Kirsten S—"

"Sawyer. I can tell by the sound of your voice. How was Italy?"

"Greece. I'm at NYU now, but listen. Something happened . . . a girl . . . she fell from a balcony in our student lounge. She was pushed—"

"Pushed? Did you see this happen? Are you sure?"

"No—yes! I don't know!" Kirsten said. "The thing is, I saw *Jones*. He's out. He was on the balcony. Why would he be there? Maybe this girl was involved in drugs. Maybe she didn't pay him or something? I don't know. But he shouldn't be out of jail—*you have to get him!*"

Peterson took a few seconds before answering. By the time he spoke, Kirsten and Lauren were on the steps of the Better Ridgefield. Kirsten's lips were shaking with the cold as she stepped into the warmth of the foyer. The place seemed empty. It looked like the whole school had rushed over to see what had happened.

"Hang on a second, Kirsten," Peterson said. "I'm getting a report." For a moment, his phone went silent.

Kirsten turned to Lauren. "This is the detective I was in touch with during the time when—"

"Hi, Kirsten?" Peterson's voice interrupted. "Okay, here's what the officers radioed in. I can't divulge the girl's name, but apparently they have a suicide note. Of course, this isn't conclusive, but I think—"

"And they haven't found Jones? They didn't say anything about him?"

Peterson paused a moment before responding. "I don't think you have to worry about Jones."

"What do you mean? He's out of jail. The only way I wouldn't worry is if he was dead!"

"Exactly."

"He's *dead*? Oh, my God. Is that what you're saying?"

"Is it possible you may have seen someone who looked like him? He's a pretty common physical type. And if he was high up—"

"Well, um . . ." If Jones was dead, then she *couldn't* have seen him. Duh. But the resemblance . . . could it possibly have been someone else? A look-alike? Maybe it was Santa Claus. At this point, in her state of mind, Kirsten couldn't trust anything she was seeing.

Can I help? Lauren mouthed.

Kirsten shook her head.

"Look, I'm so sorry you had to go through that, Kirsten," Peterson said. "It must have been rough. This time of year is the worst for student suicides. The cold. The bleakness. The grade pressure. It's all too common. *Seasonal affective disorder,* they call it."

Seasonal affective disorder?

He was so smug. So confident.

He'd been just like that when she'd reported Kyle's cause of death. Suicide, he'd proclaimed. Like he'd seen it a million times.

Kirsten and Lauren were in the dorm lounge now. Mercifully, the TV was off, leaving an eerie silence, but Peterson's voice was breaking up on the cell phone. "Not all suicides are really suicides, you know!" she said, slipping the phone from one ear to the other. "You said *Paul Stone* was a suicide, Detective Peterson! Where was *his* suicide note?"

"Kirsten, not all suicide cases leave notes," Peterson's voice crackled over the cell phone. "Stone had nothing on him. No clues. We had to piece things together forensically—"

"Not *nothing.* Maybe he didn't have a suicide note, but he did have—" Kirsten stopped herself.

A photo, she'd almost said.

But Peterson didn't know that. No one knew that Kyle had had a photo in his hand when he died—because Kirsten had taken it. And she couldn't tell Peterson about that. She wasn't supposed to *have* it. It was evidence. Stealing evidence is against the law. She wasn't even sure why she'd done it. It just sort of *happened.*

"Kirsten? Are you there?" Peterson asked.

"Um, bad signal," Kirsten replied.

"What were you going to say?" Peterson pressed.

"I—I forgot," Kirsten said.

"You saw Stone's body before anyone else did. Is there anything you need to tell us? *Is there something you're keeping from us, Kirsten?*"

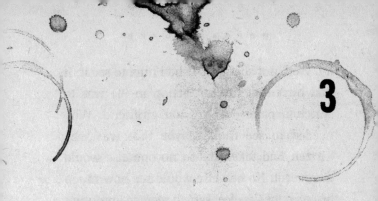

3

Soft amber light glowed

from the windows of the brick houses lining
the uptown side of Washington Square Park.
From inside, people stood watching the
snow—a tweed-jacketed man smoking a pipe,
a child holding a yellow toy truck. They were
like pictures from another era, all coziness and
warmth.

Kirsten wanted to cry.

Peterson hadn't believed her about Jones.
He'd treated her like she was a dumb kid, and
in the end, when he'd kept asking if she knew
anything more, she'd just stumbled and stammered and made excuses. Which just made
him impatient, but at least he'd dropped the
subject.

What good would it do to mention the
photo now, anyway? It was just a dumb
picture of Kyle in a bar, with Carolee—that's

all. Well, not so dumb. It had hurt to see it. It had hurt that his last action in life was to clutch a picture of his old girlfriend. Who needed to see that? Maybe that was why Kirsten had taken it—so no one else would discover it. No one else would see how much he cared for Carolee. Which seemed immature and stupid, and if she'd really thought it through, she might not have done it. But she hadn't thought at all. She'd just taken it. The point was, it didn't really matter. As evidence, it would have been useless.

After the call, Lauren had tried to comfort Kirsten. But it was already time to meet Julie, and as sweet as Lauren was, *Julie* was the one who could always make her feel better. Kirsten checked her watch. 9:02. She was supposed to meet Julie at 9:00 under the Washington Square Arch.

A cab was waiting by the curb. Its rear window slowly slid down and there she was, leaning out, waving, her sunny face framed by a halo of blond hair grown long and tied back in a way-too-mature-looking ponytail. "Hi! You look terrible!" Julie called out. "Let's do something about it. Hop in."

Kirsten opened the door and slid into the cab beside her friend. "Puerto Vallarta, please," she said to the cab driver, who returned a blank stare.

"Second Avenue and Eighty-fourth," Julie said. "The Party Room."

The cab headed west, navigating the one-way streets that would take them east and eventually uptown.

"Guess his sense-of-humor chip wore out," Kirsten muttered.

"Are you all right?" Julie asked.

"A girl just fell off a balcony and died, so close to me that I could practically feel her last breath," Kirsten said, sinking back into the seat. "Otherwise, I'm great."

The last vestige of Julie's salon tan vanished along with her smile. "Did she . . . kill herself?"

"Supposedly," Kirsten replied.

"What is supposedly supposed to mean?"

Kirsten exhaled loudly. Outside, a bicycle messenger going the wrong way swerved out of the cab's path and calmly flipped a middle finger to the driver. "I thought she was pushed," Kirsten said. "I looked up to the balcony, and near where she'd jumped, I saw Jones—or someone who looked like him. He was staring down at the body, and then he looked into my eyes—and I knew. It was Jones. The trouble is, it wasn't. Jones is dead. Peterson just told me."

"Oh," Julie said. "So, it was just someone who looked like him? Or—"

"Or what?" Kirsten asked. "Or I'm *crazy?* Yeah, maybe that's it, Jules. That makes the most sense to me. . . ."

Kirsten's voice choked in her throat. Julie was watching her with such concern, her face so open and sympathetic, and her expression brought back a flood of memories, of times when Julie was there for her—the sand-throwing bullies on the playground outside the Metropolitan Museum of Art, the humiliations of Ms. Baudry's dancing school, the junior high crushes, the horrible night after Sam died. . . . She let her body tilt ever so slightly toward the center of the seat, and Julie took the cue, wrapping her in soft, Burberry-clad arms as Kirsten sobbed.

"Sssshhh," Julie said. "It's hard coming back home. You are being so brave. Hey, awful things happen. Kids commit suicide. Frankie Federman had to be pulled back from his bedroom window after he was wait-listed at Harvard—"

"He lives on the second floor!" Kirsten said, pulling back. "And this is *nothing* like that."

"Kirsten, how far away was Jones? How many stories high?"

"I don't know. Six? Seven?"

"It's a long way up, right? No one's eyesight is *that* good. *You* think back, Kirsten—remember when you were seeing Kyle's face and Jones's face, like, everywhere? It was the pressure. Listen, you have a responsibility to yourself. To your own mental health."

"You sound like my parents," Kirsten said.

"But unlike them, *I* have your best interests at heart," Julie replied with a grin. "As soon as we get to the Party Room, I'll get Scott to pour some of his magic for us—on him. Just for fun, okay?"

Kirsten nodded.

"And guess what?" Julie added. "Sarah's home from Vassar, and Carla's coming up from Princeton. It'll be like Old Home Week."

Kirsten stiffened. Sarah Goldstein and Carla Hernandez had been two of her best friends all through grade school, middle school, and high school. They'd all cried together over Sam's death, too. But as Kirsten had stayed involved with the investigation, they'd drifted away. They'd wanted to leave it all behind. Soon, Kirsten even stopped getting e-mails and IMs from them. "Do I owe them money or something?"

"Stop it. I've talked to them both. They feel guilty. They realize they were stupid and uncaring, but they didn't mean to hurt your feelings. They know that now. They want to bury the hatchet."

"In my head or my back?" Kirsten asked.

Julie gave her an exasperated but tolerant look, and Kirsten decided it was time to glide uptown in silence, open the window, and let her own sour vibes out. She was feeling prickly, but in truth, she couldn't wait to see her old friends again.

The funky East Village streets gave way to the glass giants of Midtown, and soon the taxi was speeding up Third Avenue lane-to-lane through slow traffic as only New York City cabbies can. Somewhere above Fifty-ninth Street the neighborhood abruptly changed, and the streets were alive with kids dressed in Ralph Lauren, men still in suits walking pugs and poodles, and of course The Ladies with Face-lifts That Launched a Thousand Plastic Surgeons. Kirsten felt at home. "Welcome to the Upper East Side," she said under her breath.

As they circled around and came back down Second, Julie pointed to a small, redbrick building sandwiched between two boxy high-rises. "There," she said to the driver. "The place with no name and all the kids in front."

The Party Room didn't need a marquee or advertising—especially if you went to The Woodley School, New York's A-list prep school and venerable breeding ground for celebrity kids, old-money trust-fund babies, and Wall Street offspring. Woodley's graduating class each year was a snapshot of the future Power Elite, and at night, the Elite went to the Party Room. If you were a Woodley kid, if you knew one, if you *wished* you were one—which covered just about everyone in New York—

then you knew where the Party Room was. On the outside it looked like nothing, a relic from another time, a building too small to attract a toss of Donald Trump's bad hair. Inside, however, was another story. Inside was a cavern of perpetual good times that swallowed your cares as you swallowed some of the best drinks in New York.

Julie and Kirsten got out of the cab and ran the slow sidewalk gauntlet of hugs, kisses, "You look greats," and "How's colleges" from people they knew and people they'd never seen in their lives. If you were a regular, if you were one of the Woodley chosen, then people just knew you.

The front door was open, and Kirsten caught that familiar sweet smell of oak wall paneling and pine floorboards soaked in generations of old beer and liquor. There was nothing like it. They descended the too-steep stairs, which were rumored to have been built when the place was a stop on the Underground Railroad (and which, by ninth grade, you learned by bitter experience to take *sloooowly* on the way out). An old DMX song, driving and loud, pulsed up from below.

"We're HOME!" Julie sang, opening the door at the bottom of the stairs.

That was the door, Kirsten thought. *The door that framed Sam when you last saw her the night she'd been attacked by that Neanderthal, drug-addict ex-boyfriend, Brandon Yardley, and then left with . . . him . . . Jones . . .* Kirsten took a deep breath. *Brute Mental Force, kid. Block those thoughts. Now.* Screwing a smile onto her face, she stepped inside.

The place hadn't changed a bit. The monster speakers were tilted down from the corners, flanking a plasma TV that at the moment was showing a basketball game to a small bunch of non-dancing guys who were bellowing over a touchdown or whatever. But most of the kids were shaking and baking, interrupting themselves only long enough to give Kirsten more hugs and welcomes.

She felt better already—and twice as good when she spotted Scott, sexy and rugged as ever, behind the bar along with Kevin, the second bartender. Kirsten waved at Scott, and he smiled back, his dimples even deeper than she had remembered, which, despite the age difference between them (he had to be twenty-seven, at

37

least), nonetheless induced the great desire to get horizontal with him. It was an occupational hazard of every girl who came to the Party Room, and it got worse with each drink.

Kirsten suddenly realized that since her return from Greece, the topic of hot sex hadn't really reared its, um, head. Which was a shame. But tonight's crowd at the Party Room assured her that things were headed back on the right track.

"Some hotties here tonight," Kirsten said, eyeing a perfectly round ass that led upward to a glorious chiseled face that would have made Kirsten's pulse run wild if she hadn't suddenly recognized him as Gabe Garson's snot-nosed little brother, all grown up.

"At last, dear Lord, the girl shows signs of life," Julie replied. "Mostly high school kids, though. Personally, I am not into cradle-robbing."

"Speaking of cradles," said Scott, wiping a spot on the mirror-smooth bar top, "may I see your I.D.s, college girls?"

As usual, Kirsten and Julie both whipped out their trusty fake I.D. laminates procured one drunken evening in a shop near West

Fourth Street and vaguely waved them over the bar.

As usual, Scott pretended to look. He was already pouring. "Hey, welcome back, Kirsten. We missed you."

A pair of hands closed over Kirsten's eyes, and she recognized the unmistakable mix of chocolate and Angel perfume, which could only belong to one person. "Sarah?" Kirsten said.

"I am *soooooooo* sorry," Sarah Goldstein squealed, releasing her hands and then spinning Kirsten around. She was dressed in basic Prada, which Kirsten couldn't imagine anyone outdoing until she saw Carla in her vintage Pucci dress—and the three girls hugged and apologized and caught up and swore eternal friendship. And just like that, all four of them were up and clearing the dance floor like old times. Once again, Kirsten watched the boys' jaws drop at the flash of Carla's man-killer legs, and the bounce of Julie's devastator 36Ds, and Sarah's dance-moves-just-this-close-to-the-act-of-sex-itself. Watching the massive scramble for the best view was as fun as ever. Kirsten laughed. Some things would never change.

Out of the corner of her eye she spotted the back of a pair of broad shoulders making their way across the floor; thick, dark hair; gym-sculpted arms; a super-thin waist, with khakis; a button-down shirt; and a cotton sweater tied around his neck.

Athletic prep. Very sexy—and most likely *not* a high-school kid.

Definitely Kirsten's type these days. She danced away from her friends, accidentally on purpose bumping into the new guy from behind.

He stumbled a bit and turned. "Kirsten?" he said.

It took Kirsten a moment to recognize him. The lines of the face were thinner, the hair shorter. But the sharp-ledged brow was the same, and so was the thick-lipped grin that spread across his face like a cloudburst on a spring day. "My God," Kirsten said, "what happened to you?"

If there was any doubt, the braying-horse laugh cemented the guy's identity as Brandon Yardley. Ex-Boyfriend of Sam Byrne. Woodley's Drug King. Flunky for Jones the Dealer.

"I've turned over a new leaf," Brandon

replied. "Funny, huh? Scares the crap out of my dad. He thinks I'm pulling something."

"The last time I saw you, you were—"

"With Jones. That asshole. I can't believe what he did to me. If I ever see him again . . ."

"You won't," Kirsten said softly. "Jones is dead."

"You're kidding, right?" Brandon gave her a funny look, and a blond girl Kirsten vaguely remembered, someone's little sister, sidled up to Brandon and pulled him by his sleeve toward the door. "Oops. My public calls. See you!"

Kirsten watched them go, shaking her head.

He was wearing deck shoes, no doubt from Brooks Brothers, but *deck shoes*!

And they were paid for by drug money. Earned through a partnership with a drug dealer. Jones. The man who may have been responsible for Sam's death.

Drug money had killed her best friend, and now drug money had bought Brandon respectability. How ironic.

Kirsten suddenly wasn't in the mood to dance anymore. She crossed the room and joined Julie, who was now sitting by the bar, sipping on what looked like a very deep martini.

Scott began pouring Kirsten a drink. Kevin, the other bartender, had cranked the music up a notch, and behind them the place was going insane. In the midst of it all were Carla and Sarah, dancing up a storm.

Scott slid a lethal-looking concoction across the polished bar top as she told them all about Brandon's new look.

"Here's your Evian," Scott said. "Sip slowly, and it'll go down like water."

Kirsten took a sip and nearly fell over. "Wow. *Fire* water," she said.

"Sam was so right to dump Brandon," Julie remarked. "A shit head in Brooks Brothers clothes is still a shit head. I still can't figure out what she saw in him."

Kirsten swirled the liquid in her glass and watched it flow thickly back down the side. "Sam did not have luck with guys. . . ."

"But no more dark thoughts, remember?" Julie said. "What's over is over."

"*If* it's over," Kirsten murmured.

"Don't start, Kirsten," Julie warned. "Don't

spoil the night. The police analyzed all the evidence they had for the killings. I'm sure if they found anything else, they'd reopen the case."

Julie sounded so confident.

Maybe it was the drink, or maybe it was the encounter with Brandon—or just the nagging guilt that had been cooped up for so long. But at that moment, Kirsten couldn't keep her little secret inside. "But they didn't have all the evidence," she said softly.

Julie gave her a look. "What do you mean, Kirsten?"

"I kind of took something," Kirsten admitted, immediately wishing she could take it back.

"What?" Julie said, sitting forward and nearly spilling her drink.

Kirsten took a deep breath. "It—it was a picture, that's all. Of him and Carolee at some bar. He was holding it . . . and I took it. I—I know it was stupid, but I don't know, the picture didn't seem all that *important*."

"Do you still have it?" Julie asked. "This could be serious, Kirsten."

Kirsten downed the rest of her drink. "It's in a drawer somewhere. I haven't looked for it.

Do you think I'll get in trouble?"

"Is the Pope Catholic?" Julie replied.

Scott, who'd been busy filling an order, leaned over the bar toward them. "Hey, hey . . . let it rest," he said soothingly, sliding refills toward the girls. "What was it—a snapshot? Chances are, it wasn't that important. If you turn it in now, it'll look like you withheld it for a reason. Just between us, if I were in your shoes? I'd burn that picture."

Kirsten felt the blood rushing to her face. She hadn't meant to let Scott in on this, too.

Julie stood up from the stool. She did not look convinced. "Time to change topic. Let's dance."

Behind her, Sarah and Carla were slow dancing with a couple of guys who looked like they'd won the Lotto. An R&B ballad was playing now, a smooth Usher tune.

"You go ahead. I'll catch the next song." Kirsten turned back to the bar, where Scott was now filling a munchies bowl.

"Why aren't you dancing?" he asked. "I can see, oh, about two dozen 'Will-I-get-lucky-tonights?' salivating for you on the dance floor."

But the song was bringing back a vivid

memory. "Two summers ago," Kirsten said, absently moving some pretzels around in the bowl, "Carla's big sister's driving us out to the Hamptons in her convertible, and we get stuck in traffic—Route 27, I think—and we're *sooooo* bored . . . and *this* song comes on. Well, Sam stands up in the backseat and starts singing along at the top of her lungs, wearing only her new bikini. So like every guy for miles is gawking, and this flock of ducks waddles over from the side of the road and starts *quacking* at her, and Sam bursts out laughing and screams, 'They *like* me! They really *like* me. . . .'" Kirsten's voice trailed off, and she fought back tears. "It's a stupid story. I guess you had to be there."

"Maybe I should switch the tape," Scott said gently. "Hey, help me pick out another CD. I have a bunch of new mixes in the vault."

"Okay," Kirsten said. "Thanks."

Scott asked Kevin to take over and then he slipped out from behind the bar. Holding her drink, Kirsten followed him around the side, to the wall just before the restrooms. He took out a key and opened a locked door, revealing a deep pantry lined with shelves. On one side were liquor bottles and cartons of munchies, and on the other were stacks of CDs.

Scott handed Kirsten three of them. Most had labels written in loopy handwriting with hearts and sweet messages.

"Fans?" Kirsten said.

Scott leaned over Kirsten's shoulder. "One of these kids is into hip-hop and house, the other mix is more pop and R&B."

Kirsten held up the hip-hop CD to Scott. It was current—all new hits from this year. "Well, none of this will bring back memories of Sam, I guess."

"I must be getting old—I don't know half of these groups," Scott said with a smile. "Hey Kirsten, it's okay. Look, I know how it feels to have someone really close to you die. It changes you. Kind of turns off a light in your soul. What you're feeling is so totally normal. I can't lie to you—you will never stop thinking about her. You'll never feel the same again. But life is all about change. Slow change. You learn how to deal with stuff like this. You do. Trust me. And you move on, and life gets beautiful again—only the colors are slightly different, that's all."

Kirsten brushed a tear from her eye. Scott was such a good friend. Even if the clientele was getting too young at the Party Room, she knew she'd never stop coming here. Because of him.

As he took the CD, his fingers brushed against hers. They were blunt fingers—you would guess Macho Road Worker rather than, say, Sensitive Pianist—but the nails looked manicured, which was so *Scott.* He was full of surprises.

She caught a scent of cologne, an old-fashioned kind that she'd smelled once on Julie's hunky brother Chad, causing her and Julie to run into the bathroom and read the label, which had no recognizable designer logo but contained the words "bay rum." It was the smell of Man Unafraid, Kirsten had decided—and without even thinking, she found herself slowly inhaling, leaning toward Scott . . . and closing her eyes.

The CD fell from her fingers, clattering against the tiled floor, but she didn't care. It didn't matter what was playing. It could have been "Happy Birthday." She stood on tiptoes, and now she felt his soft, warm breath against

47

her cheeks as she moved her lips closer.

She smelled his skin now, rugged and slightly bitter beneath the cologne, and now the musky-minty scent of his breath. She felt his arms close around her, firm and comforting.

His lips were full and wide and surprisingly soft, and she could have stayed like this for hours, drinking him, breathing him, feeling his warmth course through her body, if he hadn't gently pulled away. "Kirsten?" he said.

"Mmmm," she replied, slowly opening her eyes.

He was smiling, but not the way she wanted. Something in the odd angle of his lips, the slight tightness in his face, the distance in his eyes that hadn't been there a moment ago. "Look, maybe this—"

A voice broke the spell. "Yo, Scott—this chick just asked me for a long, slow, comfortable screw against the wall! Can you believe these—"

Scott dropped his arms, and Kirsten sprang away.

It was Kevin, standing in the closet door-jamb.

"Uh," Kirsten squeaked.

"Um, I, well . . . ," Kevin said.

Scott scooped the CD off the floor as if nothing had happened. "Hate to disappoint you, Kevin, but that customer wasn't coming on to you—it's the name of a drink. One shot each of sloe gin, Southern Comfort, Galliano, vodka, and orange juice. . . ."

As the two guys left, Kirsten leaned against the wall.

Shit. Shit. Shit.

She had come on to him. Cornered Scott—good old Scott—in a closet behind the bar, in the middle of his shift, and tried to hook up with him. *What were you thinking?* she asked herself. *Ladies and gentlemen, let's give it up for the winner of the American Idiot Award.*

He was never going to look at her the same again. He knew now. He knew she was hot for him. From now on, he'd always be a little wary, a little cautious. Unless . . .

It wasn't as if he'd hated it, Kirsten told herself.

He hadn't jumped back and yelled at her. It took two pairs of lips to kiss. He'd put his arms around her.

49

Kirsten allowed herself a slightly guilty smile. It had felt good. It had felt *sooooo* good.

It was something she'd been dying to do for ages.

She composed herself and stepped out of the closet, wondering if anyone besides Kevin had noticed. The first song of the new mix blared over the speakers. Everyone was dancing now.

She jumped onto the floor, joining a group that included Julie, Carla, and Sarah, everyone moving, shaking—letting it all go. No more cares. No worries. She tossed her head back and soon she was floating, not feeling a thing except the music.

And something else . . .

Eyes.

She was being watched.

Of course you're being watched, she told herself. *You're at the Party Room. You WANT to be watched.*

But this was different. A feeling that made the hairs stand on the back of her neck. As if the crowded room had suddenly become an abandoned street, and someone was following her . . .

As she spun around, dancing, she tried to

take in the whole room, to see if anything was different and strange. The place was jumping as usual. Nothing different.

Nothing.

It was paranoia. That's all.

Relax, she told herself. *Shut out the world.*

"If I Close My Eyes" was playing now, one of her favorite tunes, drawing *everyone* onto the floor . . . Reina wailing her heart out about lost love . . .

Kirsten closed her eyes.

Click.

She swayed, swinging her hair, thinking about the new year ahead . . . about the moment she'd just spent in the back room with Scott . . . about what she'd say to him . . .

Click.

Click. Click. Click.

Her eyes sprang open at the sound. Someone ducked behind a group of dancers.

"WHAT THE *HELL?*" Scott's voice boomed across the room. He jumped over the bar like an Olympic athlete and ran through the crowd, clearing the dance floor.

"Did you see that?" Carla said. "He was taking pictures."

"Pictures?" Kirsten said. "Who?"

"What a perv," Sarah replied. "He comes up close to you, Kirsten, pretending to listen to his cell phone. Then he's holding it over you, like he's trying to see down your shirt."

Kirsten heard a guy cry out at the door. Scott had someone by the collar, pushing him, shouting into his face. She ran closer for a better look.

She recognized the orange knit hat before she saw the face—the guy from the NYU lounge. The film geek who had been taking pictures of the dead girl in the atrium. "I know him," Kirsten murmured. "He goes to NYU."

"How'd they let someone like *that* in?" Sarah asked.

"They must have had to fill a quota for jackass creeps," Sarah said.

Kirsten felt nauseated. She'd only seen this guy from behind—he'd never looked her in the eye.

Or had he?

Who was he? Why was he here? What made him think he could take pictures of her boobs?

And what was he going to *do* with those pictures?

"YOU COME NEAR HER AGAIN—YOU EVEN LOOK IN HER DIRECTION—I'LL PUT THE HURT ON YOU, BIG-TIME!" Scott boomed, grabbing the guy by the shirt and pants and throwing him upstairs.

Kirsten's mouth fell open. She had never seen Scott like this.

"Hmm . . . ," Sarah said with a raised eyebrow. "Uh, what exactly happened between you two in that back room?"

Kirsten felt herself blushing.

"Uh-huh," Carla said, and nodded. "Once a Woodley girl, always a Woodley girl. We don't miss a thing."

"Details, Kirsten. We need details," Julie said. "Did you hook up?"

"No!" Kirsten protested, unable to stop grinning. "And there are no details!"

"A likely story, given that big, fat grin on your face," Carla said.

"He's always been into you," Sarah added. "Anyone can see it."

"He *has*?" Kirsten asked.

"Duh," Carla said. "Don't play Miss Innocent."

"But if you don't want to . . . hey, I'd do

him," Julie volunteered, giving Scott an appraising eye.

"Leslie did," Sarah piped up. "She says he's great in bed."

Julie groaned. "Leslie did *not* do Scott."

"She has the condom to prove it," Sarah replied.

"EWWWWWWW!" they all shouted.

Try as she might, Kirsten could not wipe the smile off her face.

Me . . . and Scott? she thought. Hot *Scott?*

It was a concept.

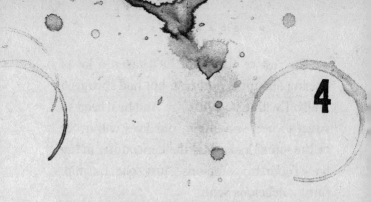

4

Kirsten floated up the front stairs of the Better Ridgefield Hotel. As she inserted her passkey in the front door, she glanced at her Movado: 1:27 a.m.

Pushing the door open, she shuddered a bit. The guy with the orange cap was in this building, somewhere. She imagined him pacing his bedroom, smarting from Scott's treatment, deciding what to say to Kirsten. But she wasn't scared. Not really. If he had the slightest reading on an IQ chart, his first words would be "I'm sorry." Better yet, he'd say nothing—ever—if he *really* knew what was good for him. Scott would be watching.

She smiled. The martini was still flowing through her, making everything seem so mellow.

Scott . . . my hero . . . She giggled a little at the thought of him.

The rest of the night he'd taken a lot of teasing about his outburst, but had shrugged it all off with a bashful grin. And he'd been so sweet to her—no funny "our lives will never be the same" looks after their encounter in the back room, no come-ons—just solid, normal, hunky, delicious Scott.

Where would this lead? Kirsten wondered. She and Scott had become good friends over the past several months, but did he care about her in *that* way? Was it possible?

Maybe. Maybe not.

Be realistic, she told herself. *Scott was there for you when you had trouble dealing with Sam's death, but you don't really know that much about him. You don't even know where he lives, or if he has a girlfriend!*

Well, whatever happened between them, Kirsten would always remember that hot moment, no matter what. Her heart thumped hard in her chest just thinking about it as she tiptoed down the hallway to her room. She unlocked room number 103 and pushed open the door, stepped inside, and flicked on the living room light.

It would take a little while to get used to the

smell. Not rotting garbage or anything. More like IKEA-type particleboard dressers and desks. They had a certain "I'm really cheap but hey that's what you get when you live in the dorms" kind of smell.

Kirsten's dad had offered to buy her a $3 million pad down in Tribecca when she announced that she'd been accepted to NYU, but Kirsten had turned him down. She'd *wanted* to live in the dorms—to be like a regular college student. So here she was, tripled up in a dumpy suite in a dumpy "hotel" with two other girls. At least the place was a decent size, as far as dorm rooms went. Most of suites at the Ridge had three or four bedrooms surrounding a small living space and a private bath, and there were a few singles scattered on the upper floors—probably reserved for seniors.

She and Lauren had nearly sanitized the room that morning, but everything looked totally different now. Piles of stuff were stacked against the walls—comics, CDs, tapes, books, camcorders, and cameras.

The New Roommate had arrived, and she was a slob.

Each of the three bedroom doors off the living room were decorated with multicolored woodblock letters: LAUREN, KIRSTEN, JAN. That was a new touch. Not Kirsten's style, exactly. All that was missing was a little needlepoint thingy that said HOME SWEET HOME. But hey, the effort was nice.

Lauren's door slowly swung open, and the dim light of her bed lamp filtered into the common room. She was dressed in a snowflake-patterned flannel nightgown, which looked soft and cozy and boxy and exceedingly ugly. Lauren's hair was loose and messy around her shoulders, her face preoccupied and grim.

"What are you doing up so late?" Kirsten asked.

"Homework," Lauren replied.

"Homework? We haven't had classes yet!"

"I got the course description for Intro to Constitutional Law. Sounds pretty neat. Thought I'd get a head start. Did you have a good time? Were you able to forget Chloe Pepper for a while?"

"Who?" Kirsten asked.

"The girl who jumped," Lauren said.

"That's her name. It was in the papers."

"Oh. Yeah." Kirsten took a deep breath. The night had been so full that she had stopped thinking about the girl's death for a while. And now the awful images were coming back, spoiling the lingering good feelings and making her feel somehow guilty, somehow disloyal to this poor girl whose name she'd just now learned.

She walked into her room and dropped her pack onto her bed. "Sorry, I guess I kind of disappeared this evening."

"That's okay," Lauren said, and exhaled. "It's been a rough day. Some way to start a college career, huh? I practically had to beg my parents to not send me a ticket home. They were horrified. The late newspapers have jumped on the story—the *Post* called it 'Sorority Sister Suicide.'"

Suicide. In a headline. That made it sound so official. As if any other possibility had been ruled out. "Do they *know* it's a suicide? I mean, have they had a full investigation?"

"I don't know. I tried not to think about it all day. I went for a swim, lifted weights, took a jog around the park. Anyway, then I got back here and found out that the movers lost my special mattress from home." Lauren pressed down on Kirsten's mattress with two hands. "Yours is much firmer than the piece of crap they gave me. I have scoliosis—I think I told you, right? You know, really bad curvature of the spine? Until they deliver my mattress, I'll deal with my futon and hope I don't do any permanent damage."

A thump sounded from the other bedroom, followed by a muffled yawn. Slowly the third bedroom door creaked open.

"Oh, that's another thing," Lauren said softly. "Our new roommate is here. Kirsten, meet Jan."

Kirsten stood up, put on her best smile, and stepped into the living room.

Out of the other room, rumpled and yawning, walked the last person on earth Kirsten had expected to see.

Jan was not a she.

Jan was a he.

And Kirsten knew exactly who he was.

Even without the orange knit cap.

5

"*You?*" Kirsten said.

She couldn't believe it.

Him. Here. Not only in her dorm.

In her room!

He was just standing there with his ravaged, "haven't figured out how to be handsome" face, looking like a little kid caught with his hand in a cookie jar.

This couldn't be happening. Not after a day like this.

"Um, I can explain . . . ," Jan replied.

Kirsten backed away, into her room. "You're—a guy. And . . . and you're . . ."

"A pain in the neck?" Jan said. "A geek? A busybody? A wiseass to Upper East Side bartenders who threaten his fragile masculinity? Guilty on all counts. Plus, I have a name that could also be a girl's name. This has not only warped me from birth, but also messed up the housing office, which is why they put me here. But despite it all, I'm kind of sweet and quirky and harmless in a loose-limbed way. And I'm a really good cook, so I do have redeeming values."

A talker. A big mouth, too-clever-for-his-own-good, talker. On top of everything else. One more notch on his belt of detestable qualities.

She hated guys like him.

"You were at the Party Room," Kirsten said. "Taking pictures. And this morning, when that girl died, you were taking pictures of *that*. Who the hell *are* you?"

Jan did a little showbiz shuffle and bowed low. "Jan deVries at your service. Worshipper at the altar of Tarantino, Kurosawa, Scorsese, Wise, and Welles, in roughly that order. My life mission: to boldly go where no filmmaker has gone before, to never stop trying to capture the essence of the human condition on film—digital or celluloid."

"Will you ever stop talking?" Lauren said.

Jan blushed. "Just tell me to shut up. I'm used to it."

"I'm going to bed," Lauren said, turning back into her room. "Classes start early tomorrow, if I can drag my aching back to them. Good night."

She shut her door, and Kirsten was alone in the room with Jan. She knew she had to *do* something, but her instincts were short-circuiting, undecided between ignoring him and shoving him out the window.

His gray-eyed gaze was darting around the room. With his left hand he nervously twirled the ends of his curly hair, which fell in knotty brown ringlets over face. And that maddened her, too, because there was something familiar about the mannerism, as if he was imitating someone she knew. . . .

"You're mad at me, right?" he asked. "You are. I can tell. I mean, there I was, being a paparazzi at the Party Room, and now here I am, in the weirdest coincidence of the century, and you feel threatened and hate my guts, and frankly I don't blame you."

"Coincidence? I don't think so," Kirsten said, folding her arms across her chest.

"No, really. I swear," Jan said. "First of all, we've never met before, right? Um. Hi, by the way." He gave a little wave and a smile, but Kirsten just stared at him. "Anyway, the likelihood of me traveling to the Party Room to see you is virtually nil. And second, you see before you a guy whose admitted misfit-loner qualities have allowed for the development of superior Web skills, for whom Googling a list of New York City hot spots is very easy—and which action would, as you can imagine, lead him to Second Avenue and Eighty-fourth Street. And once I was there, being the camera freak that I am, naturally I'd be looking for interesting subject material."

"Cell phone pictures of my tits?" Kirsten asked.

Jan turned beet-red and muttered something unintelligible about interesting angles.

Kirsten sighed. This guy was just a geek. She couldn't imagine him trying anything. And the idea of him skulking around to find the hottest club in New York—and choosing the Party Room—didn't seem so far-fetched.

She felt too sorry for him to be mad. He was annoying, but threatening? Uh, no. Probably gay, too, Kirsten figured, which was kind of a relief. "I don't exactly know how to feel," Kirsten said. "Let me sleep on this. Maybe tomorrow I can go yell at the housing office.

We were originally supposed to have a girl roommate—Clarice Moravec."

"Really? I heard she was coming here. She's famous. Did you see the documentary *Hoopskirts to Hoopsters: A History of Women in Basketball*? I didn't. Anyway, she probably got the penthouse suite at the Plaza. That's what colleges do with athletes."

"There's your great American exposé," Kirsten said, turning to go back to her room. "I get credit for the idea. Night. See you at Sundance."

She shut the door behind her and began getting ready for bed.

The fire engines blared up Sixth Avenue at around 2:15. One of the piles in the living room crashed noisily to the floor shortly afterward. A cat started wailing in the airshaft about a half hour later. Kirsten had to pee just before 3:00.

She was finally getting to sleep when Lauren began snoring . . . seriously.

Kirsten sat bolt upright. This was ridiculous. Putting on her robe, she shuffled into the living room and knocked on Lauren's door.

"Hey . . . pssst, Lauren? You're rattling windows."

She heard a series of snorts, and Lauren fell quiet. But now Kirsten was wide-awake. In the corner near the bathroom was a tiny box-shaped refrigerator that Lauren had brought. Kirsten pulled it open, took out a bottle of Diet Coke, and began pacing. *It's college life*, she said to herself. *Get used to it.*

Jan's fallen pile of junk was all over the middle of the room. Papers with tiny scratchy handwriting . . . elaborate illustrated sci-fi scenes . . . and underneath them was a manila envelope that had come open, with some photo contact sheets sticking out.

Kirsten knelt over and began neatening up. Out of pure nosiness, she pulled out one of the contact sheets. In red grease pencil, various images were circled—mostly neighborhood scenes: the West Fourth Street subway entrance, narrow little Minetta Lane, the Porto Rico coffee importer . . .

And Lauren.

Kirsten brought the sheet into the bathroom light and scanned the various images. Lauren, in a telephoto shot, descending the subway stairs (or rather, Lauren's cleavage, which was about all that fit into the frame) . . . Lauren again, lying in a bikini on a beach chair beside an indoor pool . . . Lauren lifting weights, her chest bulging with the effort . . . jogging under the Washington Square Arch . . . She looked totally unaware. The photos must have been taken over the weekend.

Guess that takes gay out of the picture, Kirsten thought as she sifted through some of the other sheets. More girls. Each sheet a portrait of some other girl, some NYU student.

Kirsten's first instinct about him had been right: a jerk. A red-blooded, heterosexual perv. Someone who followed girls around. He must have thought he'd died and gone to heaven when he got Lauren as a roommate.

Kirsten's eyes caught one of the faces— dark hair, big doe eyes and full lips . . .

She knew that face.

On a hunch, she held the contact sheet side by side with a copy of today's *Daily News* that was lying on the floor. On the front page, beneath a headline that screamed "COED

LEAPS TO DEATH," was a smiling freshman-register photo.

It matched exactly the face on the contact sheet.

Chloe Pepper.

"Oh . . . my . . . God," Kirsten murmured. He *knew* Chloe. He had been stalking her when she was alive. Then, when she died . . . *there he was.* Snapping away with his camera. And only moments earlier he'd been in the lounge, watching TV.

Coincidence?

Jan's life was a little too full of coincidences, wasn't it?

Showing up at the Party Room.

Being on the scene when Chloe jumped.

Ending up as Kirsten and Lauren's roommate.

Kirsten riffled through the sheets until she got to the last one—and she nearly screamed. There she was—Kirsten—stepping out of a cab on Fifth Avenue. Swinging with Julie on the swings in Central Park. Laughing at a corny joke that her doorman, Hector, had told in front of her house. But these were taken two weeks ago. Before she'd gotten to NYU.

Before she'd ever seen his stupid orange knit cap bobbing around the city.

Kirsten's heart raced. Who *was* this guy?

Her hands were shaking as she shoved the contact sheets back into the envelope.

She felt defiled. Violated. Sleeping in this room was out of the question. She would crash for the night on the floor of Julie's dorm room at Barnard, then make a huge stink at the housing office in the morning.

She quickly righted the fallen pile, keeping the manila envelope hidden under all the other stuff. She grabbed a toothbrush and some makeup from the bathroom, and a change of clothes from her not-yet-unpacked suitcase. Then she ducked into Lauren's room and prodded her roommate awake. "Lauren," she whispered. "Jan's been taking weird pictures. You're in a lot of them, and so am I."

Lauren sat up, grimacing. "Whaaa? Pictures? So what?"

"It's, like, peekaboo stuff—legs and cleavage. Totally sick. I'm spending the rest of the night on the floor at my friend Julie's. Come with me. Tomorrow we can go to the housing Nazis."

"Oh God, no sleeping on floors for me, but thanks. Hey, can I use your mattress while you're gone? It's much better than mine."

Kirsten nodded, and Lauren got out of bed.

"You're not creeped out?" Kirsten asked her.

"I have mace and pepper spray and a black belt in tae kwon do," Lauren replied, shuffling sleepily toward Kirsten's room. "He tries anything with me and he's toast. Night."

"I'll call you to check up," Kirsten said. "What's your number?"

"I don't have a cell. The school is supposed to give us a landline tomorrow. Leave your number on my nightstand, and I'll call you and tell you what it is."

She disappeared into the room and shut the door behind her.

A few hours later, squinting in the morning sun, Kirsten was back at NYU. It was 9:00 A.M., but she'd had only about forty-five minutes of sleep on Julie's dusty dorm floor. She and Jules couldn't stop talking all night—and Julie was full of tactical advice for what to do next.

Which was why, at this ungodly hour,

Kirsten was headed into the school athletic complex for the girls' varsity basketball team practice. Here, Kirsten intended to find out if Jan deVries really was the coincidence king.

They had found the practice schedule online. The girls, it seemed, had to practice at the crack of dawn, while the boys got a midday time slot. Figured.

Tup . . . tup . . . tup-tup-tup-tup-tup . . .

The thumping of basketballs and squeaking of sneakers on the gym floor sounded like some nightmare hip-hop track as she pushed the door open.

She focused on a girl who must have been six feet five, standing at the side of the court. She wore a knee brace and paced back and forth, shouting things like "Screen!" and "Pick off!" that seemed to have nothing to do with basketball. Her last name, MORAVEC, was emblazoned on the back of her shirt.

Before Kirsten could call out the girl's name, a big orange ball came bouncing toward her, fast. She cried out in surprise, shielding her body with her arms, and felt a sudden jolt. When she looked down, she had the ball in her hands.

71

"Nice grab," the girl said.

"Um, thanks," Kirsten replied, handing her the ball. "Are you Clarice?"

The girl's smile tightened. "Sorry, I can't do interviews during practice. I mean, I'd like to, but my coach—"

"No, no. I'm not a sports reporter," Kirsten interrupted. "You were supposed to be in my room."

Clarice cocked her head. "Are you Jan? Hey, I owe you some thanks."

"Me? No, I'm Kirsten Sawyer."

"Oh. Well, it's because of someone named Jan that I got this great single on the top floor of the hotel. So thank her for me."

"Jan got you a single?"

"Well, she gave the housing office some big sob story—she was arriving late, she had to room with someone from New York, she had a room on a high floor but was afraid of heights, blah, blah, blah. I mean, hey, it would have been nice, but I did get lucky, I guess." Spinning around, Clarice launched the basketball into the air, and it went through the hoop with a soft *swish*. "Oh, did you have something you wanted to ask me?"

"No," Kirsten said, turning away. "You told me everything I needed to know. Thanks."

She gritted her teeth and marched out of the gym. Everything she and Julie had guessed had been true: Clarice hadn't backed out of the roommate group after all. *Jan* had arranged the situation—pretended to be a girl and fooled the administration, somehow.

Coincidence, my ass, she thought.

She didn't know what Jan's deal was, but she did know something:

He was *not* going to get away with it.

6

Pot roast.

Is it weird that I like pot roast?

WHO ON EARTH COOKS POT ROAST ANYMORE?

Use "brisket cut" only, oh yes indeed, sliced thinly and on the diagonal—and if not the diagonal, pal, it SUCKS because you learned the hard way, didn't you? It's TOUGH and CHEWY that way. The slicing has to be just right, not to mention the proper searing of the meat on the bottom of the pot.

Meat . . . Flesh . . . It's all one and the same, isn't it? WE ARE ALL FLESH, AREN'T WE?

God, it's amazing how pot roast can turn you into a feakin' philosopher.

Does she think about these things?

Does she know that when you come down to it, we're all nothing but carbon and hydrogen, protein and sugar, hair and FLESH? That the only thing that separates us from an inorganic slag heap is a SOUL, and we have an OBLIGATION to that soul, and if we break it we have no privilege to keep it?

Oopsy. We're hot and ready. . . .

Into the pot goes the beef—tsssss—up comes the bubbling fat—blub, blub—and now, ladies and gentlemen, the secret blend of spices, an old family recipe . . .

Now, as long as we're being goddamn Schopenhauer here, take this cow—the one we're cooking—she had a soul once too. A MOJO behind all that MOOING. But once ol' Bessie outlived her usefulness, it was time to move on. Pot roast, baby.

Onions, garlic—tsssss—now it starts to smell. The SMELL is half the fun.

Does she know about me? About what I've done?

She MUST!

But she can't.

Then why does it FEEL that way?

Like she's on to me.

Okay, think.

THINK!

Figure out where things could have gone

wrong. *Because they shouldn't have. There was never any room for mistakes.*

I covered the bases.

Everything was under control.

SHE SHOULDN'T KNOW.

Oh, damn. Where are the scallions? I HAVE TO HAVE SCALLIONS!

Ah. Here we go. Tssssss . . .

Okay. Okay. Don't get crazy.

Make a plan. A RECIPE.

Investigate.

Give her the benefit of the doubt. For a while.

Because if she thinks she can outsmart me, she's got another thing coming.

I may be out of practice, but I still have the ability.

And the talent.

And the desire.

And the CONTROL.

And the red peppers. Always the red peppers last. TSSSSS . . .

See, WHEN I decide it's time, she goes.

And there will be nothing she can do about it.

Except scream.

7

E-mail. That had to be
how Jan had fooled the housing people,
Kirsten thought. He sent an e-mail. That way,
they didn't have to hear his voice, didn't have
to know he was a guy.

Kirsten walked into the administration
building, stomping the brown Greenwich
Village snow off her shoes, and headed for the
housing office. *Why?* Why did he do it? Was he
really that obsessed with girls? With *her?* Was
he some kind of Internet voyeur porn freak
waiting for just the right moment: "HEY,
FELLAS!!!!! CLICK ON THIS LINK TO SEE
REAL COLLEGE COEDS WALKING AROUND
TOPLESS AND MUCH, MUCH MORE XXX
ACTION! THROUGH THE KEYHOLE!!!!" There
were plenty of other girls in his pile of contact
sheets—dozens of them. He could have
chosen to sneak into any of their roommate

groups, so why Kirsten and Lauren?

The housing office was closed until ten.

Kirsten checked her watch: 9:21. She hadn't stopped at the Ridge yet to check on Lauren, but chances were good that she was already at breakfast. The thought of food made Kirsten's stomach rumble. Her appetite had come back big-time. She headed back outside, zipped her coat, and walked toward the cafeteria.

About a block away, she spotted Jan leaving the cafeteria building.

Kirsten froze. The sensible part of her wanted to run. The other part wanted to heave a block of ice toward Jan's temple. He was listening intently to his iPod, hands deep in pockets, a camera hanging around his neck.

"Hey—Jan!" she called out, but he was walking away from her and oblivious.

She had to give him a piece of her mind. Right now.

His stride was long and quick. She tried to match his pace but got stuck at a red light on Bleecker Street while he darted into the student activities building.

By the time she got into the lobby, he was gone. Above the front desk was a list of meetings and clubs: All-University Gospel Choir . . . Baha'i Club @ NYU . . . Club Anime . . . Inter-Greek Council . . . Photography Club . . .

Photography. That's why he'd be here.

On the desk was a sign-up sheet with the heading DARKROOMS. Jan's name was at the bottom, next to Room 7.

"Where are the darkrooms?" Kirsten asked.

The girl behind the desk, a serious type wearing far too much black and engrossed in a graphic novel, pointed absently to her left. "Basement," she said. "Through the door, and then downstairs."

Kirsten pulled open the basement door, stepped downstairs, and followed signs to the darkrooms. She rounded a corner to a long hallway. At the opposite end, a door flew open.

Jan barged out, clutching a stack of photos. He turned, heading toward the other end of the hall. He was picking up his work. Carla used to do that when she was in the Woodley Photo Club—leave wet pictures to dry overnight and then get them the next morning—at least until she got in trouble for locking herself and Trevor Royce in the room for *way* too long.

Kirsten ran down the hallway after Jan. She could hear him rushing up another set of stairs. But as she passed Room 7, she stopped, getting a different idea. She casually jiggled the door handle. Locked.

Then she glanced over her shoulder and pulled out her trusty American Express Platinum card from her Prada backpack and slipped it through the crack between the door and the frame. *Click.*

Too easy, she thought as she pushed the door ajar, and she made a mental note to check her dorm room lock when she got home.

Inside was a small room lit with a dim red bulb. In the near-darkness she could see a sink, a huge photo-enlarging machine, and ledges about waist-high that held rectangular pans containing foul-smelling liquid. Photos and clippings of all sizes had been taped to the wall, strips of film hung on clothespins from a line, and several stacks of accordion folders had been lined up next to the pans.

Kirsten leaned in toward the taped-up images, her elbows resting on the accordion folders. As her eyes adjusted to the light, the images became clearer. Smiling faces . . . a night in the Party Room, wild dancing, Julie and Sam and some guy Julie was seeing last year . . .

A wave of queasiness rushed through her. Just what was he doing with these pictures? How did he get them? Kirsten wasn't sure she wanted to know the answers as she stared at the horrifying collage in front of her.

Some of the taped-up images looked as if he'd photographed them himself, but many of them were old, ripped out of newspapers and yearbooks. Stuff he had carefully collected. An old yearbook picture of Sam, arm-in-arm with her old boyfriend Julian, laughing . . . Emma Lewis, flirting with Brandon, back when Emma was in her I-am-Sam's-clone phase, before she was strangled too . . . and there, in another photo, was Carolee Adams among a swarm of admirers, her head thrown back, revealing a slender, swanlike neck—the neck that had been crushed one night in the park four years ago, the grisly butchery that had started the whole chain.

"Ohhhhh." The sound escaped from her throat as she stared . . . stared at the happy, smiling pictures of girls who were now dead. She tried to sort it all out. Clearly, Jan was a freak. That's why he had lied his way into her room. But, why? What was he going to do? Did he have some crazy plan that involved her?

She moved on to another set of familiar faces. Talcott kids she vaguely recognized who'd long since graduated—a group of friends and a kid with thick brown hair who could only be . . .

Kirsten squinted. *Kyle!* Back before he'd gone to jail. Back when he was a student at Talcott.

Was Jan so obsessed with the murder case? Fixated with the thing that had torn her own life apart? Some wackos collect famous people's shoes—Did Jan have a "Preppy Murder" fetish? That had to be what this was all about. And the fact that she was rooming with him made her ill.

Kirsten backed away from the wall. A topsheet from one of the accordion folders had stuck to her elbow, and she pulled it off: ADAMS MURDER, it read.

She turned the folder open-side up and skimmed through the yellow legal sheets with handwritten notes, more newspaper clippings and photos—all related to Carolee's murder. She glanced at the labels on the other folders: BYRNE MURDER, LEWIS MURDER, AUTOPSY PHOTOS. Sick.

Kirsten lifted the last folder. Swallowing hard, she looked at the top photo.

It was Sam.

Sam. Naked and ghostly pale, her eyes open as if daring the photographer to shoot, a blue bruise over one side of her face and her soft beautiful auburn hair matted by blood.

It was Sam. Dead.

Kirsten let out a gasp and dropped the folder, let it fall on the counter, spilling out more images of her best friend, side, front, close-up, full-body. And the obvious questions of *How did he get these?* and *Why does he have them?* and *Who the hell is this freak?* were lost in the jangled sparks that were short-circuiting her brain.

As she backed out of the room, the images on the wall seemed to taunt her with their frozen smiles, the four faces circled in red grease pencil . . . Sam . . . Emma . . . Carolee . . .

All the dead girls. He'd circled all their faces. Plus one—one other face that Kirsten hadn't noticed before, circled bold and thick.

She ripped it off the wall for a closer look. And in the first split second of recognition, her mind's chaos rallied into a stubborn wall of denial, trying to convince herself that the face *wasn't* circled, because it made *no sense* for this face to be circled, only *dead* people were circled and the person *inside* the circle wasn't dead, but as alive as . . . as . . .

. . . as she was.

It was *her* face.

Her own face marked like the others. Circled. Like a target.

Carolee . . . Sam . . . Emma . . . me, she thought. *Marked for death. Like the last in a line of victims.*

"No . . ." The sound welled up from deep within, hoarse and rasping. She clutched the photo to her chest, not wanting to let go of it, as if taking it away would prevent her own . . .

Her own what?

Murder.

She turned, pulled open the door, and

lunged for the hallway. But she couldn't go far. A tall figure blocked the door.

Jan.

"Out of my way!" Kirsten crouched, leaning her right shoulder into Jan's chest.

He gasped, leaping back into the hallway. "What the—?"

Kirsten tore off toward the staircase.

"Wait!" Jan shouted.

But Kirsten was taking the stairs three at a time, racing across the lobby, scattering visitors and students. She burst out onto the street, still holding the photo, nearly falling on a patch of pitted ice. She didn't stop until she reached the housing office. It was open now, and a mild-looking lady with cat's-eye-shaped glasses sat behind the reception desk. "I need to speak to the freshman housing person," Kirsten said breathlessly.

"You'll have to sign up for an appointment," the lady began.

"Don't tell me to wait. I will not leave until you have given me a new room!"

A couple of surprised faces peeked over cubicles, and the lady rose quickly from her seat. "Let me get someone who can help you."

She disappeared into an inner office for a moment and then stepped out, gesturing Kirsten inside, where a balding man dressed in a tweed jacket looked up from a computer.

"I understand you have a conflict," he said with a tight smile, "and I sympathize. But I'm afraid it is late in the year, and roommate groups are no longer as fluid—"

"My roommate's name is Jan deVries," Kirsten interrupted, trying desperately not to shake, "and he's a *guy*. Somehow, you let him room with two girls. But, what's worse, he's a pervert and possibly a murderer—and if you don't switch me, I will have the police on you before you can say 'tweed coat.'"

The man tilted his head as if trying to decide if Kirsten was crazy. "These are serious accusations."

Kirsten placed the photo—the one she'd taken from the darkroom—on the man's desk. "He did this," she said.

The man leaned forward—and Kirsten immediately realized what an idiot she was being. It was a picture of her face, circled in red. Out of context, it meant nothing. "I got it in—" she began. In where? A darkroom that she broke into, raiding someone's private materials? How would she explain *that?* "Never mind," Kirsten said.

"Well, he has a good photographic eye," the man said noncommittally, then began tapping on his keyboard. "You are right. You shouldn't have a male roommate. That is actionable. But, as I suspected, the database is coming up blank on open rooms. There's quite a crunch. Look, I will talk to Jan and see if I can get him a temporary transfer—and I'll put in an expedited request for a single for you next week. That's the best I can do," he said, handing her a sheet that read, REQUEST FOR ROOM TRANSFER.

Kirsten took the sheet. Her hands were shaking.

"We're very sorry," the man said with a wan smile. "It was a clerical error."

By lunchtime, Kirsten had been to French and Intro to European Art History but hadn't retained a thing. The words *clerical error* had taunted her all morning. She could see the headlines now: "College Coed Killed in Clerical Error."

The guy at the housing office had treated her

like crap—like she was just another pesky, dreary kid. And so had Peterson, when she'd called him.

He's about had it with my phone calls, Kirsten thought. *He probably thinks I'm a certified nutcase by now.* She sat in a corner of the cafeteria, facing the door in case Jan came in, fiddling with a plate of congealed pasta al pesto. She was so distracted, she didn't even notice when Lauren slid into the seat next to her.

"Hey, how was Barnard?" Lauren asked. "Meet any neat-looking Ivy League guys?"

Kirsten jumped. "You scared me. You're still here, thank God. You'll never believe what I found out about Jan."

"I think he likes you," Lauren said, setting down her tray.

"*What?* Oh my God, don't say that. You have no idea what you're saying—"

"He's not so bad," Lauren said. "And he was a perfect gentleman last night."

Kirsten felt sick to her stomach. "That sounds like something from an old movie. What was he a perfect gentleman *about*, Lauren? You and he didn't . . ."

"Do it? Oh, please, no!" Lauren said with a funny giggle.

"Because if you ever get that idea into your head, if you ever even think about it, I will personally drive you back home to Kansas—"

"Wisconsin."

"Whatever. Look, he is worse than any of us imagined. . . ." Kirsten carefully went through every detail of her discoveries in the living room and the dark room, plus her encounter with Clarice Moravec.

Lauren listened closely, sipping from a bowl of split-pea soup. "That *is* kind of icky."

" 'Icky'? It's a little more than that, Lauren," Kirsten said.

"Okay, but I guess I'm not so sure why you're *so* freaked out," she said. "I mean, let's break it down. Let's look at it objectively. He likes to sneak pictures of girls. That puts him in a big club with, like, oh . . . the majority of guys I know. Besides, I knew he was taking those pictures of me. He was kind of obvious."

Kirsten raised her eyebrows. "You *knew?* And you didn't kill him?"

Lauren smiled. "I kind of enjoyed it," she admitted. Then she tilted her head. "Does that make me an exhibitionist or something?"

"Uh, *yeah,*" Kirsten said.

"Really?" Lauren's face fell. "Is that bad? I posted some pictures of me on the Web, too. On this dating site."

Kirsten was seeing her roommate in a new light. "Like, *sexy* pictures?" she asked.

"Um, I guess it depends on what you call 'sexy,'" Lauren replied with a sly grin.

Kirsten groaned. Pure little Lauren the Lawyer wasn't as innocent as she seemed. "God, Lauren, one kinky roommate is bad enough, but *two*?"

"Look, let's stay on point here. I do think it's strange that he circled the faces. That's kind of weird. But did you look at all the pictures? Are you sure there weren't *more* faces circled, faces that didn't fit the pattern? I mean, photographers like to mark their best images with circles—for cropping, for reproductions. Did you *really* look? Did you go back and rule out all the possibilities?"

Kirsten couldn't believe this. Lauren sounded as if she were deciding a case for the Supreme Court. "You couldn't pay me enough money to *ever* go back there. And you wouldn't do it, either, if you saw a copy of your best friend's autopsy photo."

Lauren grimaced. "That must have been so awful to see. He probably got it over the Net, you know. People do that. Once, when I was doing a report on the Civil Rights era, I found the autopsy photos of John F. Kennedy, with, like, half his head missing. He looked like he was smiling. *That* was weird."

Kirsten dropped her fork and held back a sudden small upsurge of half-digested pasta. "Please, Lauren."

"What I mean is, I'm thinking that Jan may be doing some kind of project. Something involved with the murders. That's why he's collecting all that stuff. I mean, he *says* he's a documentary filmmaker, right? So it would make sense."

Kirsten nodded. It was a reasonable explanation. But it didn't really hang together. "The thing is, if he was shooting a documentary, why would he keep it a secret from me? He could just ask me for info. But, instead, he goes through all that devious stuff to room with us!"

Lauren thought about that a moment, then sat up with a start. "Oh! Speaking of Jan, I almost forgot!" She reached into her pocket and pulled out an envelope. "I saw him on the way here. He told me to give you this note."

"A note?" Kirsten said warily. "What's in it?"

"I didn't ask," Lauren replied. "Read it."

Swallowing hard, Kirsten opened the envelope. Reluctantly she unfolded the note.

Kirsten,

I know what you took.

We need to talk.

Do NOT, under any circumstances, show or tell anyone what you saw.

Or we are both dead.

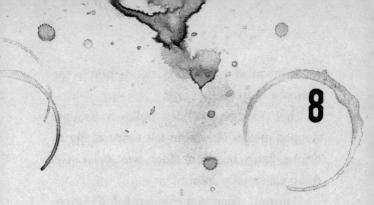

8

"Uh-oh," Lauren said ten minutes later, unlocking the door to their room and peering inside. "He bounced."

"He's *gone*?" Kirsten said, though she really wasn't so surprised.

Lauren pushed the door wide open. All of Jan's stuff—piles of papers, and suitcases, and books—had disappeared.

"See what I mean?" Kirsten said. "He's running scared. You read the note. 'I know what you took . . . we are both dead.' How do you explain this, Counselor?"

"Maybe the housing office cleared him out. What did you tell them—that they put you together with this generation's Charles Manson?"

Kirsten shook her head. "Not quite. The guy didn't believe anything I said about Jan, anyway. He said he was going to *talk* to Jan.

Made it sound as if he'd be taking him to the Plaza for high tea."

Their footsteps echoed hollowly as they stepped inside. The room felt twice as big as before. Jan's bedroom door was open. His room was totally empty.

"Lauren, when you saw Jan before lunch, did he say anything about this?" Kirsten asked.

"Nope. But he was in a rush. I guess he was in the middle of moving. God, this *is* starting to get kind of creepy." Lauren walked into Jan's room and tried the mattress. "Ugh. Soft. How come *you* got the only good one?"

"Now what?" Kirsten asked, sinking into the living room sofa with a deep sigh. "Am I back to looking around corners, into shadows?"

"Kirsten, I admit, if I were you—if I'd seen what you saw, and if I were as close to the murders—I'd be on the first plane home," Lauren shouted from the other room. "This is totally weird. But my gut tells me this guy wouldn't hurt a mosquito. You've spoken to him. You know what he's like. 'Don't tell anyone, or we're both dead. . . .' This is a guy who probably scripts his life dialogue from bad movies. Hey, at least we don't have to room with him anymore."

Kirsten paced, trying to settle, trying to think *straight*. Lauren seemed so rational, so feet-on-the-ground. But Lauren wasn't the one who'd gotten that note.

"We need to talk . . ."

Talk about what? What did Jan mean? And when were they supposed to talk? *Where was he?*

Lauren walked out of the cleaned-out room with a smile. She put her hand gently on Kirsten's shoulder. "I have an idea. You need some R&R, I need to find an ATM, and we both need to celebrate our expanded room situation. So how about taking me shopping for a new image?"

This was *not* what Kirsten had expected at a time like this. "Um, I gave you a new image already. Or at least some practice getting one. And there's an ATM on Sixth Avenue."

" 'ATM' as in, 'rich boyfriend.' Like, M-I-T—Mogul in Training? Don't tell me you didn't know that?"

"Uh, yeah . . . but I'm not exactly thinking about *shopping* right now," Kirsten said.

"I thought you always thought of shopping!"

Lauren said, smiling. "Look, Kirsten. Don't let Jan ruin your life. If he wants to talk to you, he'll find you. Then we can both give him a piece of our minds. Meanwhile, my parents sent me some money, and I want a neat new look—like, all-American but sexy. I want guys' eyes to pop out when I pass by." She grabbed her shoulder bag and headed for the door. "So if you don't want to come with me, fine. I'll just have take myself to Joyce Leslie. Where's the mall in this town, anyway?"

Kirsten took a deep breath. "I may be totally screwed up about my life, Lauren. I may be hallucinating and seeing conspiracy theories and misjudging everybody. But I will *not* allow you to go to the mall. Wait up."

Henry Higgins.

That's who Kirsten felt like. The guy from the old movie musical *My Fair Lady*, who rescues a girl from the gutter and teaches her how to dress and talk.

Well, it wasn't that extreme. Lauren was upbeat and optimistic and so enthusiastic about clothes—and after a while, Kirsten actually began having fun. *Much* more fun than old Henry H. ever did.

Gently convincing Lauren not to use the word *neat* was Step One. Getting her a decent pair of jeans—a pair of low-rider Sevens from Intermix—was Step Two. This was made difficult by the fact that on the way out she kept trying to pull the jeans up, asking, "Can you see my butt?" every few feet and not accepting "That's the point!" as an answer.

Giggling like kids with their first credit card, they ducked into Stella McCartney's place in the meatpacking district, Anna Sui in Soho, and Barneys uptown—just for ideas—and then they zoomed to the trendy stores on the Lower East Side so that Lauren could buy the same styles at half the price.

By the end of the day, Lauren had her outfits organized into Smart Tart outfit, Future Big-Bucks Attorney outfit, Keep-It-in-Your-Pants-I'm-Not-Interested outfit, and last but not least, her Slut outfit. Plus, a handful of cute, sexy camisole tops that Lauren didn't want to buy until Kirsten forced her.

They celebrated with a CD-buying spree

and Frappuccinos at Starbucks, and then cabbed it back to the Ridge.

As they entered the dorm with armfuls of bags, Lauren said, "There's nothing like spending money to cure all ills."

"I never thought I'd hear you say that," Kirsten replied, bursting into the suite and dropping her shopping bags onto her bed. "Yeah, I feel human again too."

"So, what about dinner?" Lauren called from her room. "What should I wear? Something really neat. I mean, *hot.*"

"Definitely one of those camisole tops," Kirsten suggested. "You will never have to worry again about sleeping alone. And I hear sex is great for your back."

Lauren lifted one of the tops from her collection. It was a soft, sexy, honey color, and paper-thin silk. "I . . . I can't," Lauren said, suddenly shy.

"Why?"

"They're too . . . nippular."

" 'Nippular'? Is that a word?"

Lauren shrugged. "It is now."

"Nipples, my dear," Kirsten said, "make the world go round."

Lauren howled with laughter, and Kirsten found herself laughing too. Big, free-and-easy, just like she used to.

Nothing was right about her life these days. So much needed to be figured out. But for the first time since returning from Greece, Kirsten had the glimmer of a feeling that maybe—just maybe—things could work out.

And it felt good.

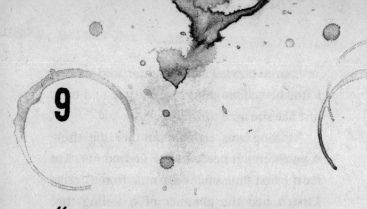

9

"She convinced you this guy was harmless?" Julie asked, reaching across the bar for a handful of pretzels. "After all those freaky pictures? And you actually went with it?"

Kirsten took a sip of her Cosmo. The Party Room was pretty quiet, as was usual on a Monday night. Brandon, looking like he'd popped out of a J.Crew catalog, was dancing with a Gwyneth Paltrow's-little-sister type, whose face was starting to betray Stage Three of the Five Stages of a Relationship with Brandon, which included Attraction, Doubt, Disbelief, Anger, and How-Could-I-Have-Been-So-Stupid?

Kirsten had come in there in a decent mood, calmed down by her spree with Lauren. But the mood was starting to fade. Julie's reaction was a rude shock into reality. "Lauren is very convincing," Kirsten said. "She is going to make one kick-ass lawyer."

"Did you go to the cops?" Julie asked.

"Yup. They treated me like I was reporting a jaywalker. The housing office, same. But at least Jan is gone from the room. That's a good thing. Oh, here's that picture I was telling you about." Kirsten reached into her bag and pulled out the shot from the darkroom.

Julie looked closely. "Why'd he circle your face?"

"He also circled other faces in other photos—Carolee's, Sam's, Emma's . . ."

"Oh, you've got to be kidding. That is so morbid. You don't need to call the cops, you need to call a psychiatric facility. I can't believe he did this."

Scott leaned over the bar with a raised eyebrow. Kirsten felt suddenly warm all over, and she couldn't help a huge smile from taking over her face. A dozen clever, sexy opening lines formed in her head, all jockeying for position, but they all got stuck, so she opted for, "Hi, Scott."

"What's that you got?" he asked, nodding at the picture in Julie's hand.

"You'll never believe it," Julie said, starting to hand it over to him.

Kirsten grabbed the picture. "Forget it. You don't want to know," she said. Actually, she didn't think Scott needed to get involved in this. He'd already had to deal with too much of her drama since she'd come home, and it wasn't fair.

"Aw, come on. You guys know I don't allow printouts of Internet porn in here," Scott said with a sly grin. "Unless you share it."

"Oh . . . my . . . God," Kirsten murmured. She put the photo back in her pack, slowly watching an orange hat moving through the crowd until it turned into Jan.

"Who's that?" Julie asked.

Kirsten was already off her stool and halfway across the floor, headed for Jan. "What the hell are you doing here?" she demanded. *"What was that note all about?"*

"Oh. Hi, Kirsten," Jan said nervously. "Sorry to spoil your night, I didn't want to come here, especially if Conan the Barbarian Bartender is on duty, but we have to talk. Look, you didn't have to go to the housing office. I can explain everything."

"You can explain what? Autopsy pictures

of Sam? What do you do with them, Jan? *What do you do with pictures of dead girls in the darkroom?*"

At Kirsten's outburst, a group of kids jumped away.

"Shhhh . . . listen, it's not what you think," Jan said.

"Oh. That's right. You like live girls, too. I guessed that when I saw the pictures of Lauren's breasts. That must be why you fooled the housing office and forced them to get rid of Clarice. You could keep all your little fetishes alive—sleep in a suite with two *live* girls and hey, it gets better. One of them knows all the *dead* girls you've been salivating over. You need help, Jan. You're *sick!*"

"Look, I did a stupid thing, I admit. It's this cinematic technique of mine. Total immersion. I believe a filmmaker has to be close to his subject. Live and breathe the same air. I'm a . . . student of the Byrne killing. I recognized your name in a list of the incoming class. I believe serious crimes need serious film studies—not like that awful TV movie Hollywood made."

"That is the biggest crock I've ever heard.

You're a serious student of NYU, Jan—not the Byrne killing. Sam Byrne doesn't need a wacko like you poking around her autopsy photos and spying on her friends. You . . . you get your skinny ass out of here right now, and if I ever see you again, I swear I will make your life miserable."

Now Julie was by Kirsten's side, taking her hand tentatively. "Is this the guy?"

"Look, Kirsten," Jan pleaded, "after what you did to me this morning, you could at least listen. You and I . . . we want the same thing. The trouble is, you don't even know it. And if you don't wise up—if you don't listen to me— you are going to be in deep shit. Trust me."

"Don't you threaten her!" Julie said.

"What do you mean, 'after what I did to *you*'?" Kirsten shouted at Jan.

Scott emerged from behind her, his jaw set firmly. "Yo, my man, I thought we had a little talk last time. Did you forget?"

Jan nodded, backing away. "Nope. As I recall, you told me to get out of your bar, I told you it was a free country, and you replied you would give me a free kick in the balls if I ever came back."

"Guess it's time to collect," Scott said, grabbing Jan by the collar and pushing him toward the exit.

"Maybe we should finish our drinks and go," Julie said, gently leading Kirsten back to the bar.

By the time they got there, Scott was charging back in. He swung around behind the bar, his brows furrowed with anger as he began mixing drinks.

Kirsten felt awful. His life must have been so much easier when she was in Greece. "Sorry, Scott," she said. "I hope you're not mad. I mean, after all this time, I'm rubbing your face in the drama of my life all over again."

Scott's tense expression eased. "Hey, how can I be mad? It's not your fault. All beautiful girls have hangers-on like that guy. He'll disappear."

Kirsten found herself blushing when she heard the word *beautiful*. Not that it was the first time a guy had paid her a compliment— it's just she had never heard it from Scott. But this was no time for a crush. "But this guy is fixated on Sam—on the whole murder case.

He says he's making a film. So I feel like it's *not* over. Like, I came back to New York and it's all starting again."

Scott leaned over the bar and touched her hand. It felt warm and comforting and strong. "It *is* over, Kirsten. It has to be. All of this stuff happened in the past, and you have to move on. The killings have stopped. Paul Stone—*Kyle*—is dead."

The words hit her hard. "Kyle doesn't really have anything to do with it, Scott. Remember? We talked about that."

"Right, right . . . I know," Scott replied gently. "Sorry. Look, I know how you felt about the guy. Really. But I've been thinking. Since he died, nothing has happened, Kirsten. No murders. You have to consider that. Now, I know some of those cops on the case. They're smart guys, and they're convinced. I'm sure Stone was a great guy, but he was pretty screwed up, too, right?"

Kirsten turned away, fighting back the impulse to scream. But she couldn't be mad at him. He didn't know. He was trying to help. "No offense, Scott," Kirsten said, "but you didn't know him like I did."

"Well, that's the truth," Scott replied. "I'd never met him except for that one time he came here and started talking to you. And yeah, from what I remember, he did seem like a pretty normal dude. It's just that . . . you never *know*, Kirsten. People aren't what they seem sometimes. He *was* picked up for that other murder, all those years ago . . . and two times is pretty serious, don't you think?"

Kirsten realized she must have inadvertently been giving him a poisonous look, because his voice trailed off and he smiled apologetically. "Sorry," he said. "I'm just a dumb bartender. Friends?" He leaned over the bar, arms open.

Kirsten fell into them, fast and hard, feeling his strength and tenderness, not caring who saw, not caring what kind of exaggerated juicy description Julie would give Carla and Sarah. If she could, at that moment, she'd make it every bit as juicy and more.

He gave the best hug, long and enveloping, lifting her out of her gloom and squeezing all the bad feeling away. Every pore tingled, alive and open. She felt caring and cared for, safe and protected.

"Ahem," came Julie's voice from behind her.

Kirsten let go and sat back on her stool, and Scott's smile looked so delicious she could hardly keep herself from jumping over the bar and wrestling him to the floor. "Friends," Kirsten said, answering Scott's question.

"Um, sorry to break up this little love fest," Julie said with an arched eyebrow, "but I believe we had a plan."

Right.

Julie and Kirsten had spoken earlier in the day. The idea was to start out at the Party Room and barhop through the night, hitting all the newest places on the East Side. "My coach turns into a pumpkin," she said to Scott. "See you soon?"

"You're leaving?" Scott said. "I—I'm getting off soon. I thought maybe we could . . . talk."

Kirsten gave Scott her sexiest smile. She wouldn't mind talking with him . . . and whatever else he had in mind. But Julie was already halfway out the door. "Maybe we can get together another time?" she asked, hoping she wasn't hurting his feelings. "I promised Jules that I'd go to a new place with her tonight." Scott nodded, and she slung her bag around her shoulder and paid for her drink. "See you later," she said, and headed toward the door to meet Julie.

When they reached the sidewalk and turned south down Second Avenue, Julie asked, "News?"

"No news," Kirsten replied.

"Come *on*," Julie said. "That was the hottest hug I have ever seen between two fully clothed people. Kirsten, *what* is going on with you two?"

"Nothing! I mean, just what you saw. We hugged. I like him. That's never been a secret."

"Girl, if there was any doubt in my mind that the feeling was mutual, that little incident just proved me wrong." Julie gave Kirsten a sly smile. "Umm, look, do you *really* want to do this? Because I could go ahead to the Yellow Trance *alone*, if you want to stay and . . . you know, hook up."

Kirsten laughed. "Yellow Trance?"

"Brand new. Verrry hot, says Carla. And just around the corner."

Actually, all Kirsten wanted to do was turn and bolt back into the Party Room and hang out with Scott, but the "I don't really want to go alone" look in Julie's eyes was too much to ignore. "I'm there."

They walked a couple of blocks downtown. A crowd of kids spilled out of the Yellow Trance entrance, which was on the ground floor of a sleek, black high-rise. It was an upscale, part-Euro crowd, lots of thin smokers dressed in black outside, speaking French and Russian and Japanese, with Afro-Cuban dance music blaring out whenever the plate-glass doors opened, which was often.

"Different crowd," Kirsten remarked.

"I think I heard some people speaking Greek," Julie said. "It'll bring back all the right memories."

Kirsten threw back her shoulders and headed for the front door. The bouncer unhooked a velvet rope, and the two girls entered. The bar was just inside the door, a huge slab of marble that stretched practically to the back of the place, where another door opened to a garden. It looked great, but Scott's drinks had worked their way into Kirsten's bloodstream, and the sudden rumbles in her stomach and whirls in her head meant that the first order of business would be the restroom. "Be right back," she said to Julie, who returned a knowing glance.

A group of guys, so hot looking it almost hurt Kirsten's eyes, were laughing and toasting one another at the bar, and she squeezed past them, running directly into a couple—older guy, younger girl, both dressed in black—who were slurring their words and looking totally tanked.

The girl staggered away to let Kirsten by, yanking at a halter top at least two sizes too small, and babbling incoherently. The guy was oblivious and unmoving.

Jerk, Kirsten thought, an observation reinforced by the fact that he was wearing a beret—a *beret,* how was that for a lapse in taste?—not to mention the shaved head, which Carla said was usually a sign of "sexual dysfunction guilt," only God knows how Carla would know.

"Excuse me," Kirsten said loudly in his ear as she passed, noticing the red roots that he hadn't had the good sense to shave before showing himself in public.

"Sorry," he said in a strange, gravelly voice, moving aside.

Kirsten bolted for the bathroom—then stopped in her tracks.

Red roots.

Red roots meant red hair.

Lots of people had red hair. But not too many of them shaved it all off. And spoke in that voice.

She knew him. She knew who he was.

Swallowing back the lump that filled her throat like a tennis ball, she turned back toward the bar.

He was throwing back a drink, laughing. And she got a good, direct profile.

The slightly droopy eyes and thin lips. The tiny scar above his right eyebrow. The super-broad shoulders.

How could it be? Peterson said the man was dead.

But there was no question now. This was up close, personal, and totally clear. Peterson was wrong. Jones was not dead. He was right here—as alive as she was!

Kirsten opened her mouth to call for Julie, but the name jammed in her throat—because he was turning . . . slowly . . . scanning the room like a vulture looking for a corpse.

Until his hawklike eyes met hers.

Idiot.

Fool.

I should have known it was too good to be true.

They never learn. Every time you think they do, they prove you wrong. They wave their stupidity in your face like a flag.

I've been watching her closely. Too close for my own good.

And now she KNOWS. Face it.

And she's stupid enough to try to DO SOMETHING ABOUT IT.

Okay then, fine.

She doesn't want to PAY ATTENTION? Fine.

She can't see what happens to the ones who mess up? Fine.

She wants to make me work hard—as if I haven't done enough, as if I hadn't taught all those lessons, put out all those fires? She thinks that's easy? FINE! FINE! FINE! I'LL DO IT!

But it's such a waste.

I thought she was one of the smarter ones. I thought I didn't have to worry about her.

Ah, well.

She's insisting, isn't she? So what choice to I have?

I'm a reasonable man. I believe in honoring people's desires.

I'll give her what she's asking for. Ashes to ashes, dust to dust.

I will be quick with her. It's the best way.

Part Two

Part Two

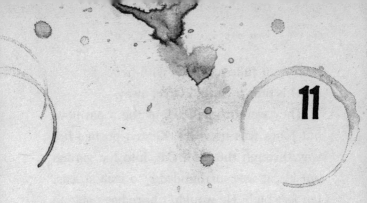

11

"JULIEEEEE!"

A dozen people spun around in surprise, a dozen more jumped out of the way. Julie came charging through, her eyes wide. "Kirsten? What happened? Are you all right?"

"He's . . . he's . . ." She pointed toward Jones. But he was gone. *"Did you see him?"*

"Who, Jan?" Julie asked.

"No, Jones!" Kirsten said, pushing her way through the crowd. "He's here. Follow me."

She raced to the back of the room. She would track him down. Now. *With* Julie—not like last time. Last time, when he'd had long hair, when she'd caught him at a different bar, asked him about Sam, and he'd run from her. Kirsten had chased him—alone. She'd found him on the street and managed, somehow, to wrestle him to the pavement. But he'd gotten away. He was stronger. If Kirsten had only had help . . . if Julie had been with her . . .

This time he wouldn't get away.

They were in the back of the room now, but Jones was nowhere. Kirsten pushed her way through the back exit, into the garden outside. It was surrounded by a wall at least ten feet high. He wouldn't have been able to climb over it—at least not without creating a huge commotion.

She paused in the doorway, looking around. The tables were half full. Knots of people stood chatting and laughing, drinks in hand. They circulated around, examining everyone's face, checking the shadows.

Nothing.

"Maybe it was someone who looked like him," Julie suggested.

"I am *over* seeing people who don't exist," Kirsten said firmly. She'd been there—seeing Kyle and Jones around every corner, in every shadow and footfall, raising paranoia to a 24/7 art form—and Julie knew it. But that was before Greece, back when Kirsten was interning at radio station WXRJ during the day and abusing substances at night. She was steady now, if not totally sober—and Jones was Jones. Kirsten could not have been more sure. "Trust me on this one, Jules. He was as close as you are. He recognized me. I could tell. And he ran. I don't know how he got away, but he did."

"You have to call Peterson right away," Julie urged her.

"Peterson is the one who told me Jones is dead," Kirsten said. "He won't be any help. I'll have to get Jones myself!"

"Kirsten, don't delude yourself. He's a drug dealer, at least. Maybe even a murderer," Julie said. "We can't play hero. It's too dangerous. Talk to Peterson again tomorrow. *Convince* him that you know what you saw."

Kirsten exhaled. "Okay, okay," she said, knowing Julie was right. The adrenaline was draining from Kirsten's body, and up rushed the nausea she'd had when she came in. Only now it was worse. "I'll be right back," she said. "I—I'm not feeling too great."

"Do you want me to go with you?" Julie asked.

Kirsten managed a weak smile. "I stopped having nannies in sixth grade."

"Eighth, for me. I never got over the scars

of humiliation. Hurry back, okay? I'm worried about you. And I won't be able to hold back the hotties at the bar all alone."

Kirsten adjusted her shoulder bag and stumbled to the restroom. It was empty, thank God, but the place smelled of leftover vomit and tangy disinfectant, which didn't make her feel any better. She went into the stall and closed the door. Phone numbers and crude anatomical drawings were all over the walls, and a metal toilet paper dispenser, sturdy and once intact, lay on the floor, empty and twisted.

Kirsten leaned over the toilet, which was—thankfully—clean.

Breathe . . . breathe . . . She wasn't going to puke. She *hated* puking. It was her least favorite human activity. *Mind over matter. . . . Keep it in. . . .*

Yes. The feeling was going away. Slowly. And Kirsten began thinking about Jones again. Julie was right: She would have to report him to Peterson, convince Peterson of his existence, somehow.

But what was Jones doing *here? Tonight?* Jones was a dealer. Was he looking to sell drugs?

Or looking for me? She swallowed back her

nausea and leaned against the wall. It was too confusing. *Rational. Be rational. Look at the big picture.*

He—or someone—had killed everyone associated with Sam's murder. Everyone except Kirsten.

Now Kirsten was back. In school. In New York.

And there was Jones, on her first day of freshman year . . . killing again. Killing someone who'd had nothing to do with the murder.

Why Chloe? Was she a random victim— was it just a coincidence that Kirsten had been in the atrium when Jones pushed her? And also a coincidence that he was there tonight?

No. Kirsten didn't believe in coincidences anymore. He had to have planned it all. He had to have known Kirsten would be in these places. Which meant that Chloe's killing might have been a signal. *He might have pushed Chloe to warn me—to say, "This could happen to you."*

But why? Why would he sacrifice an innocent girl when he could have gone after Kirsten himself? Was it some kind of game? Could he possibly be that sick?

Calm down, Kirsten. You came in here to feel better. You feel better. Now take a few breaths. Put yourself together. And get out of here. She inhaled deeply, ignoring the stink. One . . . two . . . three . . .

Click!

The bathroom door opened, and Kirsten froze. Had she locked it? No, she hadn't. She'd been in too much of a rush. In another moment she heard the door shut—the quiet *thunk* of the doorknob lock . . . the rattle of a hook-and-eye gizmo.

She would wait until the person washed her hands or snorted her coke or whatever she'd come in here to do. The door of the stall rattled.

Kirsten jumped. "Someone's in here," she called out.

The rattling stopped for moment. And then the light went out.

"Hey, turn it on! I'm still in—"

She heard the stall door yank open, felt the subtle suck of stale air from the stall. Before she could stand up, an arm grabbed her around the neck. And a hand closed over her mouth as she screamed!

12

"Whfff . . . ," she mumbled,
but the hand was thick. Strong.

A guy.

Instinctively she opened her eyes wide, but
there was no light. She couldn't see a thing.

He was pulling her down toward the toilet,
grabbing at her purse.

*My bag. He wants to strangle me with the
strap. He's going to kill me!* Kirsten felt her
knees buckle. She was sinking toward the
toilet. She pushed back, but he was strong.
Relentless. She reached out, grabbing for
something, *anything*.

Her fingers closed around a thick piece of
metal. The broken toilet paper dispenser.

She swung it up, over her head—slammed
her attacker hard.

Thwack.

Contact.

She heard a startled groan. The grip loosened.

"Yeeeahh!" she grunted, swinging harder.

Thwack.

"Arrrrggghh! " he cried out.

She stood up, pushing hard with her thigh muscles. Her attacker fell backward, and she heard his head hit the tiled wall. Kirsten turned, reaching back with the twisted metal dispenser, but he shoved her aside, bolting out of the stall and through the bathroom door.

She straightened herself out, her hand dripping blood from clutching the jagged metal, and she dropped the dispenser. Holding the bleeding hand with her good one to stanch the flow, she staggered out into the dim light of the Yellow Trance.

There he was. Running through the crowd, pushing people aside, making a commotion. She caught a glimpse of a black shirt, an arm pushing someone aside.

Jones!

"Stop him!" She ran, ignoring the blood, pushing her way across the floor.

In a moment, Julie was by her side, alarmed and confused. "Kirsten, what happened? Are you okay?"

"Did you see him?" Kirsten shouted, not breaking stride. "Did you see Jones? He attacked me! *Don't let him get away!*"

He was racing out the front door now. She couldn't really see him, but she could tell where he was by the sudden movement of the crowd he was pushing aside. Then a gap. She could see a dark figure barging into the crowd on Second Avenue, running off to the left.

"Please! Somebody, stop him!" Kirsten shouted into a sea of blank, seen-it-all New York faces. She was out the door seconds later. But she ran straight into someone who had decided to step right into her path.

"Get out of my—" she began. But the words caught in her throat as she glanced up into Jones's face. "Ahhhhh!" she shrieked, jumping back and falling into Julie, who staggered backward, grabbing on to the edge of an outdoor table.

Jones took off at a sprint, up Second Avenue.

The same direction she'd seen him run just seconds before.

"That's him!" Kirsten shouted.

"How could that be him?" Julie said. "He ran away!"

Kirsten balanced herself and took off in pursuit. Jones was already to the next corner, picking up speed. Another figure was halfway up the next block, farther away, running even faster.

Jones was chasing him.

Wait. What's going on? Kirsten wondered. *Who is he chasing? The guy who attacked me? Because if it wasn't Jones . . . then who was it?*

13

"Hi, Lauren?"

Kirsten settled back into the Ralph Lauren sheets on her four-poster bed, cradling her cell phone in her shoulder. Her window looked out across Fifth Avenue at the darkened hulk of the Metropolitan Museum of Art, its roof glowing faintly with moonlight reflected off a dusting of snow.

She and Julie had totally failed to find Jones—or the other guy. As usual, Kirsten had reported the incident to Peterson, and he had gone through the motions—asking questions, giving reassurances. But she didn't expect anything to come of that.

She'd needed some stability tonight, some good, old-fashioned TLC. Which was why she'd come home for the night.

"Hi, Kirsten?" Lauren's slightly groggy voice replied. "What's up? Still shaking your booty?"

Kirsten smiled. Hearing the word *booty* from Lauren's mouth was, in some weird way, unbelievably uplifting. "I'm staying at my parents' house tonight."

"House? You live in a house?"

"Okay, *apartment*. 'House' is a figure of speech in New York." *Well, sort of,* Kirsten thought, considering that her family's 4,032-square-foot Fifth Avenue duplex was probably twice as large as the average house in Sheboygan and about fifty times the price. "I—I couldn't face going back downtown after tonight. I was just at a bar with Julie and—well, there was some trouble."

"Which is a figure of speech for . . . ?"

"I kind of got beat up," Kirsten admitted.

Lauren's voice rose an octave with alarm. "Are you all right? Is there anything I can do? What happened?"

"Yes, no, and it's a long story," Kirsten replied, "which I promise to tell you tomorrow, when I get back. But don't worry. I'm fine. Well, mostly. My left hand is not so happy. Look, I just wanted you to know where I was—and if you want to use my mattress again tonight, feel free, okay?"

"Thanks, I'm already sleeping on it. Well, I'm really glad you're all right, Kirsten. That's the most important thing." Lauren let out a sigh of relief. "Hey, I almost forgot. You got some good news. The housing office called. Tomorrow they're moving you to a single. I'm getting two new roommates: Ralph and Harvey. Actually, that's a joke. Two girls . . . *real* girls."

"I'm getting a single?"

"That's what you wanted, right?"

"No," Kirsten said. "Living all alone is *not* what I wanted. I like rooming with you. I just wanted them to replace Jan with a girl."

"Did you tell them that?"

Duh. She hadn't told them. She'd complained about Jan to that stuffy housing guy, and that was it. "Um, I think I blew it," Kirsten said. "Maybe we can room again next semester?"

"Only if you continue to take me shopping *this* semester. I have to keep up appearances."

Kirsten smiled. "Deal."

They exchanged good-byes. Within a half hour Kirsten was home, turning off her bedside lamp. But as soon as her face hit the pillow, her eyes zinged open.

A single? In a decrepit former SRO, among a school full of total strangers? Maybe she'd have to grovel to Tweed Man again. She tried to push the thought aside, tried to force herself to sleep.

Through her double-pane casement windows, which were supposed to be sound-proof, she could hear the muffled whizzing of taxis—and then the slurry voice of Frankie Federman's younger brother Chip as he got out of a limo, no doubt back from some deb ball . . . and then the flapping of wings that could not possibly have been a pigeon but was more likely one of the famous Fifth Avenue hawks returning to its nest behind a land-marked gargoyle with a tasty meal of fresh-killed rat for its offspring . . .

Stop it! Kirsten silently shouted. *Sleep!* And then she heard a thump in the front hall and leaped so high, she nearly hit the fabric draped over the posters of her bed.

Clank.

Was someone trying to get into the apartment? She slid out of bed and opened her door, hoping to hear the sound of Dad padding out of his room. But no such luck, so she tiptoed through the apartment, across the living room, hoping to get there before whoever it was actually managed to . . .

Thwack!

What was that? It came from the kitchen. Which was totally dark.

Kirsten leaned toward her parents' bedroom and called, "Dad . . . Mom?" but her voice was swallowed up in the brocade and swags and down sofa pillows and built-in oak bookshelves filled with signed first editions, and she was running now, across the living room, through the parlor with Dad's pool table, cursing the *bigness* of the place—as a low whistling started . . . and then a sweet, high-pitched voice singing in Russian . . .

Kirsten stopped in her tracks. It was Sasha, the night porter, collecting the trash.

Easy, Kirsten. Calm down. She fell into one of the antique chairs, giddy with relief—and way too edgy to sleep. At another time, before Greece, she would have gone straight to the bathroom and fumbled for her mom's endless supply of Ambien, but not now. Not anymore. *You're home . . . you're safe . . .* she chanted to herself.

She stood up, yawned, and slouched back

to her room. Her closet door was ajar, and she shuddered involuntarily. The last time she'd been so scared in her own house, she'd found someone's muddy footprint in her closet. That print, of course, turned out to have been Brandon's, back when he was in one of his drug-addled phases, sneaking into people's apartments. But she had been totally freaked by that . . . and for a while, she thought the print might have belonged to Kyle—Paul Stone—the guy everyone thought was Sam's murderer. And *that* was the thing that had scared her, because for a time, she had believed it too.

Kirsten plopped down into bed and felt a jolt of guilt. Why had it taken so long to give him her trust? Because she'd been swayed by the news media, that's why. Because she was too scared to really listen to him. To *believe* in him. And if she had—if she'd helped him instead of cut him off when he really needed her, *when the killer was closing in on him*— maybe he'd still be alive. Maybe he'd be in her life right now, a living, breathing person instead of the way she remembered him now, lifeless and cold, his eyes vacant. . . .

In a horrible rush, it all came back, as if she were there—the mustiness, the metallic smell of blood . . . her own moaning, a sound so otherworldly, she hadn't even realized she was making it . . . his blood seeping into the floor of the dingy hotel room he'd been hiding in . . . her own shaking fingers grabbing the picture he was holding and, slipping it in her pocket . . .

The photo. The one she took from him.

It was here. In her house. Somewhere.

The memories were unfolding, from the place they'd been locked in her brain . . . the photo . . . yes, she'd been aware of it when the police came to the crime scene, when they took her away for suspicion of his murder . . . in her frantic, desperate mind she'd been thinking *don't search me, don't take my only memento* . . . and they hadn't. They'd asked her questions, questions that for the life of her she couldn't remember, and the next thing she knew, she was home, totally cleared of any wrongdoing, lying in bed with Mom and Dad hovering and an arsenal of prescription drugs on her night table. She was in PJs, somehow having changed, and the outfit she'd been wearing was draped over her desk chair, to be washed by Marisol, the morning maid . . . with the picture still in the pants pocket. She was aware of that, she was dying to see it, she *had* to see it—*yes, now she remembered*—and when she was finally alone, she'd dug it out of the pocket for one last glimpse of Kyle alive . . . but the image of him and Carolee, looking so blissful, was like a stab in the chest, causing her to moan so suddenly and so loud that her mother came rushing back from the other end of the house, so she quickly got rid of it. . . .

Where?

In a plastic bag. She had grabbed a pharmacy bag from the floor, left from the drugs, and quickly wrapped the photo—and then, quickly, she'd hid it . . . hid it where no one would know . . .

In the back of her closet!

Yes. Under the mahogany wardrobe.

She ran into the closet—her pride and joy, which was the size of some kids' entire bedrooms—and knelt by the stately antique on which she had painted the words THIS WAY TO NARNIA as a little girl. And as she pulled away boxes and bags that had collected around the legs, she wanted more than anything else to dive inside and find herself by a snowy streetlamp in the land of a witch and a lion, because the idea of actually finding the thing she was looking for scared the crap out of her.

Her fingers closed around a thin plastic bag and she dragged it out. *Lotos Pharmacy.* This was it—exactly what she'd been looking for. The picture Kyle had been clutching when he died. With unsteady fingers, she unfolded the bag and pulled out the small snapshot. Along the white border were tiny flecks of brownish red she hadn't noticed before— *blood, Kyle's blood*—and she touched them, feeling both repulsed and somehow calmed, intimately connected with him.

The image was still sharp and bright—a bar, with lots of people in it. People she knew, much younger than they were now. Maybe four years younger. But Kirsten's eyes went directly to the two faces front and center— Kyle and Carolee.

Carolee. Kirsten had never met her. But she had recognized her from the news articles about the first murder that surfaced after Sam's death. The smiling, painfully beautiful yearbook photo that had appeared daily in the newspapers. It was the same person—Kyle had good taste—and in the picture he was holding her tight. His hair was thick and unkempt, like the old photos of him in those same news articles. Their faces were flush, their smiles ecstatic. As if they'd just had sex. Or maybe it was just their tans. That had to be it. The tans.

He was in love with her. Did he ever smile like that around me? Did he carry a picture of me with him too—or was this only one? The image SO IMPORTANT that he had to grab it as the life drained out of him—to gaze at her one last time.

Kirsten felt a wave of disgust and guilt. They were dead. Both of them. How stupid to be feel jealous!

She should have given the photo to Peterson. But it was too late now. Tears streamed down her face as she slumped back to bed, propped the picture on her nightstand, and wondered how the hell she would sleep tonight.

14

Sam.

Emma.

Carolee.

Mmm, nice photos. BEAUTIFUL GIRLS.

Yes.

*Look at them. Look at them closely, pal.
Because for what comes next, YOU HAVE TO SEE
THEIR PAMPERED, AREN'T-I-FABULOUS
FACES!*

Yes.

*Because this work is not easy. Oh God, is it not
easy.*

*But the pictures help. Because they're a
reminder.*

Yes.

BEAUTY IS FLEETING.

A goddamn profound cliché if I ever heard one.

*Well, you come by it honest, oh yes you do.
You discovered it yourself. Someone close to you.*

IT'S NOT FUN WHEN SOMEONE CLOSE TO YOU—SOMEONE WONDERFUL . . . BEAUTIFUL—IS SNUFFED OUT.

An eye for an eye, The Man says.

DOESN'T HE?

YES!

Okay.

Okay. You're ready. You can do it. Put the pics away.

And, um, separate Sam and Emma, will ya? Emma was weird. Don't want her to do anything scandalous. Put Carolee between them. She'll make sure they behave.

Now. Move. It's time.

Time for the next one.

The LAST one.

Go.

Before you get cold feet.

This will be the hardest.

She should know how good she had it.

You've been giving her such a chance. Just watching.

You've been handing it to her. And what does she do?

HOW DOES SHE SHOW HER GRATITUDE?

You never should have let down your guard.

But you did.

You gave her the benefit of the doubt, and LOOK WHAT HAPPENED.

It's been too long, that's the problem. Too long, and you're out of practice.

You had a taste for this. You had technique. CONTROL!

Your problem is kindness.

You should have known she'd be trouble. You should have gotten her long ago. Invited her up for some pot roast and a life lesson. Once upon a time you would have thought of that. Before you got rusty and soft.

Before YOU LOST CONTROL.

Well, no more Nice Guy.

Open door.

Step outside.

Fasten your seat belt.

It's Time.

15

"I don't care what you *think* you can work out with the housing office," said Gil Sawyer, Master of the Universe and, oh yes, Kirsten's father, too, as he pulled his cell phone from inside the breast pocket of his black Paul Stuart suit jacket. "I will not have you continuing to live in a former flophouse. I will not have you living in any building that does not have top-level security."

Kirsten slammed down her spoon, causing the kitchen table to shake and her granola to spill over the side. After last night's miserable sleep, she was in no mood to be bossed around. She had told her parents about Jan over breakfast because she'd had to. The jerk at the housing office had called to report the room change, and Mom and Dad had greeted her this morning with a demand to know *exactly* what had happened. Kirsten had tried to tone it down: All she said was that Jan was a guy who had fooled the office into thinking he was a girl—but that was already enough to drive Dad ballistic. Kirsten hadn't even mentioned a thing about last night in the Yellow Trance bathroom—and her claim that a stovetop burn had resulted in the bandage on her hand had been accepted without question.

The fact that Kirsten had roomed with a guy, however, was serious. *That* got Dad into Mover-and-Shaker mode.

"Listen, Dad, I can handle this," Kirsten said. "I don't want to live off-campus, like some rich freak!"

"Hot cocoa?" her mom asked as Marisol, the morning maid, set a steaming cup and a plate of whole-wheat apple-walnut waffles on the table. "Go ahead, have some breakfast, sweetie. This is a fragile time for you. Your father wants you to have peace of mind. It will feel good to live in a full-service building—at least for a semester."

"Get me Ed Spencer at Cloverdale Realty," Dad was saying over the phone. "Coop, condo, doesn't matter . . . high floor, view . . . have him slip something to Martinetti at Butterfield

Movers, because I need four men today, including anyone he knows in IT."

"I guess *my* wishes don't count, when they stand in the way of Gil Sawyer, Hot-Shot Lawyer!" Kirsten blurted out.

Her father put his hand over the receiver. "But these *are* your wishes, aren't they? You didn't want to live alone in that rat trap. You said so."

"I know—but can't you work WITH me? Can't you at least conference me in with the university so I can have some say—so I can live with real kids instead of half-dead businesspeople in a museum?" Kirsten bolted up from the table, put her granola bowl into the sink, and stormed off. Her father paid lip service to Quality Time, to Getting to Know Your Daughter, to Teaching the Values of the Well-Examined Life. But as a dad, he hadn't exactly been hands-on. When things went wrong, he fell back on the only things he really knew how to do well—wheeling and dealing. Denying that the word *no* existed in anyone else's vocabulary but his own.

"Kirsten?" her mom called out. "Kirsten, do you have cash for a cab?"

Kirsten grabbed her pack from where she'd left it in the living room, walked into the vestibule, and pressed the elevator button. "Why doesn't Dad just call the Taxi and Limousine Commission and buy me a fleet?" she said as the door opened and she disappeared inside.

She regretted using the subway the moment she went down the stairs. The MetroCard machines were all busted, and a hysterical guy with a potbelly and Coke-bottle glasses was cursing out the booth clerk, holding up a line that snaked almost up to the street. People in business suits were awkwardly jumping the turnstiles, shouting, "Already paid!" or "Weekly!" or "Monthly!"

Finally she squeezed onto a Number 4 train next to someone with garlic breath, which she had to politely endure during a ride that seemed to last for months—and then, after transferring to the 6 at Union Square and exiting at Astor Place, she had to walk clear across 8th Street to the west side, which this morning felt like a ten-mile hike.

By the time she entered Washington Square

Park, Kirsten was already late for her first class. She felt like sleeping, not rushing to retrieve her books and run to class. The snow had melted, and as she hurried diagonally across the park, the city trees looked spindly and forlorn. The sound of a siren broke the stillness, and Kirsten watched the flashing light of a police car make its way around the park.

It turned onto the Better Ridgefield's block.

Kirsten squinted. The street already contained a few sets of flashing lights, but they'd been obscured by a crowd of people who had gathered at the corner of MacDougal Street. She picked up her pace, emerging from the park near the chess-for-pay players who seemed oblivious.

"What's going on?" Kirsten asked a student who was hanging on the outskirts of the crowd, but got only a shrug in return. She pushed her way through the gawkers. Soon she could see an ambulance directly in front of the Ridge. The front door was open—and a team of EMT workers was carrying away a stretcher on which a body lay, covered head-to-toe with a sheet.

Kirsten blanched.

When someone on a stretcher was injured, you saw their face. When the face was covered, that meant they were dead.

Someone had died—in her dorm.

Oh, God, she thought. *Another jumper? An overdose? Why? Why is it that wherever I go, people die . . . ?*

Where was Lauren? She wished Lauren had a cell phone, so she could know what had happened.

As she walked warily to the building, watching the EMTs lift the body to the back of the ambulance, a police officer eyed her warily. "Sorry, miss, you have to stay back."

"I—I live here," Kirsten said. "Can't I go inside to my room?"

The cop gave her a look and signaled to another officer, who was standing by the back of the ambulance as the body was loaded on. As he approached Kirsten, she read his name tag: SERGEANT P. FOLEY.

He held what looked like a purse. "You're a resident?"

"Yes," she said, suddenly feeling her legs start to shake.

Sergeant Foley nodded. "If you don't mind,

can I ask you some questions?" he asked, pulling something from the wallet.

Kirsten tried to speak but couldn't.

The sergeant held an I.D. card toward Kirsten. "Did you know the victim?"

She didn't recognize the face at first, or the name, because her mind was shutting down, telling her it was time to turn tail and leave, hop a plane and fly to Greece—no, *beyond* Greece, to circle the world again and again, passing the international date line each time so that she could go back in time, way back, to before any of this ever happened. . . .

And maybe she would avoid the horror of right now, of staring at a laminated card that had a smiling photo and a name she knew all too well.

Lauren Chaplin.

16

"There must be a mistake!"

Kirsten said, looking toward the body, which was now being strapped into the ambulance. "Can I see her? *Can I see her face?*"

She didn't wait for an answer, running to the stretcher, hoping that it was a mix-up, that it was someone else, *anyone else*—but Sergeant Foley took her arm, pulling her back.

"I'm sorry, miss. It is the same person as the photo. She was a friend?"

"She's my *roommate*! I just talked to her last night! She was fine. She was in bed. How did this happen?"

"The perpetrator managed to break into her bedroom while she was sleeping—judging from the wounds, maybe five, six hours ago," Foley said. Then, he added, as if to comfort Kirsten, "Most likely she didn't even wake up."

"Wounds? What kind of wounds?"

"A blunt object. To the head. And she was stabbed several times. As I said, she was sleeping—"

Kirsten felt light-headed. The street seemed to rise up to her in a spiraling fog. It was happening again.

The same thing.

The exact same thing.

"Tell me about her wrists," Kirsten said in a shaky voice, fearing the worst. "Were they tied up? With a school tie or something?"

The sergeant gave her an odd look. "No. Nothing like that."

There should have been something on the wrists. The killer had used the tie on Carolee and Sam . . . and he'd tied Emma with a T-shirt—Kyle's shirt.

Was this a different killer? Think, Kirsten, think.

The tie hadn't been used on Kyle, either. The ties and shirt had been a sign. They had been used to frame Kyle. But it didn't matter anymore. It no longer meant anything.

Kyle was dead. The killer was free to kill any way he wanted.

But why? *Why Lauren?*

She was killed five or six hours ago. It was about 9:30 now, so that would have been around 4 a.m. Kirsten and Lauren had talked around 2:00. *Two hours before the murder.* If Kirsten had come back instead of going home last night . . . if she'd been there . . .

A couple of other police officers had joined Foley at her side, a man named Trezza and a woman named Olsen. All three of them were leading Kirsten into the building now. They were asking questions, looking her straight in the eye, and she nodded back numbly but didn't hear a word.

The carpet outside the room had been sprinkled with talcum powder, covering Lauren's spilled blood, and a team of detectives was dusting for prints on the door frame. Kirsten and her three escorts stepped over yellow police tape and entered the room.

Lauren's bedroom door was ajar, but the cops were in Kirsten's room, searching around.

My room. Of course. Lauren was sleeping in my room tonight, not hers.

And a dark realization squeezed her like a fist.

If the killer wanted Lauren, he would have

149

gone to her room. Her name is over her door. But he didn't. He went in and headed straight for the door labeled KIRSTEN.

"Oh, my God . . . ," Kirsten said, sinking onto the living room sofa.

"Miss Sawyer?" Officer Olsen said.

The killer wasn't looking for Lauren. He was looking for me.

Sergeant Foley crouched next to her. "Did someone have anything against the girl?"

"An ex-boyfriend, maybe?" Officer Trezza asked. "Someone who held a grudge? Someone who knew her daily routine?"

Not a grudge against her. Against me.

I was to be his next victim.

If I'd come back instead of going home, I'd be on the stretcher, headed for the morgue.

The next in the line of murders—Carolee, Sam, Emma . . .

The faces passed through her mind.

The faces . . .

Circled in red . . .

Kirsten's mind flashed back to the photos, the contact sheets pulled against the wall. He had marked her.

The police wanted to know about a

grudge? *Jan* had a grudge. Big-time. And Jan had the key to the room.

It was all becoming clear. Jan's act at the Party Room last night—the apologies, the sheepish look—all bullshit. He was tracking her. Scott had pissed him off by kicking him out. So Jan had marked time. Waiting. Planning. He'd had his chance at Yellow Trance, but he hadn't counted on Kirsten being so resourceful. So he waited some more, figuring that Kirsten had gone back to her dorm room. He could try again, no problem.

And so he'd sneaked in, unseen by anyone. And why not? No one suspected him besides Kirsten. Not even Peterson, who was supposed to help her.

And now her beautiful, sweet roommate was dead.

Why? Because busy Kirsten had been uptown . . . leaving Lauren unprotected . . . because no one had taken precautions, *not even the detective assigned to the case.*

"The asshole . . . ," Kirsten muttered through clenched teeth, slowly standing up.

"Miss Sawyer?" Foley asked.

"I want Peterson," Kirsten said.

"Who?" Trezza asked.

"Focus, Kirsten," Olson urged. "Your statement right now can help us."

"I will give a statement," Kirsten said, heading for the door, "to Detective Peterson, at the Eighty-eighth Precinct."

It didn't take much time to get to the Upper East Side when you were running red lights in a cop car with a siren and flashers.

At the precinct house Kirsten got out of the backseat and barged inside while the other cops were still hauling themselves out.

Peterson was standing against the back wall, sipping coffee and chatting with another officer. He looked like Brad Pitt after a few too many doughnuts, and his slate blue eyes traveled right to her bandaged left hand. "What happened to you, Kirsten?"

"Never mind that," Kirsten said. "There was an attempt on my life in my dorm room, my roommate was killed, and I need to speak to you."

"I just got the report," Peterson said with a heavy sigh. "I didn't realize it was your room. I'm so sorry, Kirsten."

"I am too," Kirsten replied, feeling the pressure of tears behind her eyelids. "It's easy to be sorry. But Lauren is dead—and she was in my bedroom, *using my bed,* which means she died instead of me. You could have prevented it. I told you about Jan deVries, Detective Peterson. I told you about those creepy pictures—*and you didn't listen!*"

She couldn't keep it inside any longer. On their own power her fists rose toward Peterson's chest, and she didn't care that he was a cop. She wanted to break that smug expression, make him suffer, make him hurt the way she'd hurt. . . .

He moved so fast, she didn't even see him grabbing her wrists quickly, firmly. She was locked in position, arms up like a praying mantis, and as the tears began to flow, the other officer shrank away and Peterson gently led her to a small office off a green-tiled hallway.

Inside, he offered her a chair and a box of tissues. "Kirsten, I know how you must feel. And I assure you I *am* taking this seriously. I know about deVries. The faces circled in red. The threatening letter. We're running a full background check on him. So far, all we've been able to find is the transcript from NYU—honor student, Wetherby, Massachusetts—nothing unusual. But the high school has a tough privacy policy, and they're not even taking our calls, so we're working on it. Meanwhile we *have* been taking you seriously, Kirsten. We've been tailing him—not 24/7, but enough."

"Obviously not enough," Kirsten snapped. "Obviously not last night. *He had the key to our room!* Who else could it be?"

Peterson leaned over his desk, turning around a pad of notes so Kirsten could read them. "The killer didn't use a key. The report says the lock was broken."

"Broken?"

"One good solid rap, at just the right angle, and these things snap. If deVries had a key, chances are he'd have used it."

Kirsten scanned the note . . . *blunt object . . . forceful blow . . . twenty-three stab wounds . . . great strength . . .* "If he didn't do it," she said, "then who did?"

"That's what I want to know. Think, Kirsten. Is there anyone else? Anyone you've seen who's been acting suspicious? Trailing you, maybe?"

"Of course I have!" Kirsten couldn't believe her ears. Had he forgotten all the phone calls? What kind of detective was he? "Jones. Jones. Jones. I've told you! Chloe Pepper. The back room at Yellow Trance!"

Yellow Trance. It felt like ages ago, but it was just last night. A few hours before the murder. Kirsten sank slowly back in her chair. Maybe she was right the first time. Maybe it *was* Jones who had come for her—not Jan. Jones knew she was an NYU student because he'd seen her in the atrium. And finding her room information couldn't have been hard. She sighed. Jan . . . Jones . . . this was all so confusing. Why couldn't Peterson bring them both in and figure it all out? Why did it seem as though Kirsten was the only one taking this thing seriously?

Peterson shifted uncomfortably. "Um, Kirsten, I told you, Jones is not in circulation. Let's take Jones out of the discussion."

Kirsten nearly jumped across the desk. "That's what you said last time. You're wrong. I saw him at Yellow Trance. He was as close to me as you are now—closer! *How can you explain that?*"

Peterson's eyes suddenly darted away, looking toward something through the doorway, out into the hallway.

Kirsten followed his glance. A man dressed in black was heading toward them down the narrow corridor, walking fast, his shaved head reflecting an eerie olive green in the fluorescent lights. Jones—he stopped in mid stride, just outside Peterson's office, when he saw her. His black jacket billowed out, revealing a holstered gun on his belt.

Kirsten stood up, her body stiff with fear. She watched, frozen, as he reached across his chest and pulled out . . .

. . . a badge?

Kirsten's heart nearly stopped. "You're . . . a *cop?*" she said.

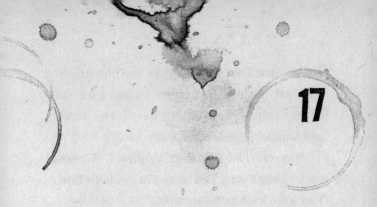

17

Jones stepped forward,

his body now filling the doorway. He was clean-shaven, his slouched posture now ramrod straight, his druggy eyes sharp.

"Sergeant Albert Russo," Jones said, extending his hand for a shake. "I believe we've met. Don't be afraid. I'm a detective."

Kirsten thumped backward against the wall.

"A detective," she said, turning to Peterson. "You told me he was dead!"

"Not exactly," Peterson said. "I just didn't deny it when you asked. I had to. I had to protect him. He was undercover at the time. Narcotics."

"Oh, God," Kirsten said under her breath. "You have got to be kidding."

"You know, I've always wanted to tell you what a bruise you gave me a while back—around the corner from Janus?" Russo said. "I mean, yeah, I was doing the slo-mo druggie act because I was working to find the neighborhood dealers—but your tackling me on Eighty-third Street was one of the more embarrassing moments of my life."

"Dealers like Brandon Yardley, " Kirsten said. "That's why you were always with him. You were manipulating him."

All Brandon's stories rushed through her mind. Jones was a BIG dealer . . . Jones had gone to jail but had been sprung, and he'd come after Brandon . . . demanding payment . . .

"Brandon was a good source," Peterson said. "Russo was using him to get to the big guys who were operating at the New York private schools."

"The kid was petrified I'd blow his cover to his dad," Russo said. "Big-shot Wall Street guy—all kinds of stuff named after him, including the Yardley Library. Anyway, the kid helped me break a drug ring—and he and I came to an agreement. He's on his way to rehabilitation, and I've been checking up on him."

"Which is why he's cleaned up his act," Kirsten said absently. She looked up. "And the night you left the Party Room with Sam?" she asked. That story was coming back to her, too.

"Sam thought Brandon owed money to *you*. You were demanding he repay his debts, and she was trying to help pay it back. *That's* why she left with you the night she died, isn't it?"

Russo nodded sadly. "It was hard keeping the secret from her. I always managed to convince her not to pay. That night she seemed so confused, so angry at Brandon. I offered to take her home, but she refused. Said she could get there on her own. She didn't want to be seen with a drug dealer like me. I couldn't blame her. I should have insisted. If I'd only stayed with her a little longer . . ."

His voice trailed off, and Peterson picked up. "Anyway, Sergeant Russo has moved on to homicide. He always felt close to the Byrne case, so he managed to get the assignment—over my objections. I figured you'd run into him and recognize his face, but he thought the shaved head would do the trick." He gave Russo a raised eyebrow. "Sergeant Russo is a stubborn man."

Kirsten nodded, her mind in a flurry of thoughts knitting together months of misunderstandings. "So the day Chloe Pepper fell . . . when you were up there, on that balcony . . ."

"I'd been checking up on you—just

routine," Russo said. "When she jumped, I ran up to see if there'd been foul play. But it was a suicide, Kirsten. The girl had been depressed and never went to see anyone about it."

"And at the Yellow Trance?" Kirsten said.

"I've been keeping an eye on this deVries guy," Russo replied. "Not that we've found anything, but you've had some serious complaints, and we're having a hard time tracking his records, so you never know. Anyway, I got a tip he was going to the Party Room, but by the time I arrived, he was gone."

Kirsten thought back to the struggle in the bathroom—the strength of the attacker, and Jan's skinny body. The attacker had seemed big, but how could she know? It was dark . . . and sometimes a person's strength could be deceptive. "So," Kirsten said, "you think the attacker in the bathroom was . . ."

Both men fell silent.

Russo pulled up a chair and sat down heavily. "Tell me some more about this deVries kid," he said.

The familiar Jackson Hole late-night crowd was soothing to Kirsten. She needed soothing after a day like this. And food. She hadn't eaten since her mom had forced a lame turkey sandwich on her this afternoon. The visit to the precinct had destroyed Kirsten's appetite.

It was just after 10:00 P.M., and it had been hell convincing Mom and Dad to let her go out with Julie. All of a sudden, in their minds, she was twelve years old again. What was worse, Dad had announced that the movers were already taking her stuff out of the Ridge and into the building on lower Fifth Avenue, where the average age hovered around, oh, eighty-two. But she hadn't been able to get angry. All day she'd been haunted by thoughts of Lauren. The Chaplins were scheduled to fly in tomorrow to collect her things and take her body home to Wisconsin to prepare the funeral. What could she say to them? It was because of *Kirsten* that the killer had broken in. It was because of *Kirsten* and her decision to sleep at home that her bed was empty, which was why Lauren had been sleeping in it . . . and was murdered. How could she face the Chaplins? Would she ever get over her guilt? She didn't think even a thousand sessions with her therapist, Dr.

Fitzgerald, would help her get over this.

Kirsten took a small bite of her Woulia Boulia salad and holding her fork delicately in her undamaged right hand, she watched Julie inhale a Santa Fe burger. "Where do you put it all?" she asked.

"With some people, it goes right to the thighs. With me, I swear it must go here," Julie said, shaking her 36Ds, "thereby also feeding the fantasy lives of Woodley boys, Columbia students, and men of all ages."

A fork clattered to the floor nearby, and a red-faced boy stooped to pick it up.

"It's hard being in public with you sometimes," Kirsten said.

"A lot of things get hard when I'm in public," Julie replied with a sigh.

Kirsten smiled. Julie was the only person who knew how to cheer her up when things were really bad.

"Now, tell me what happened after you met Officer Soprano this morning," Julie said.

"Russo," Kirsten corrected her, taking another small bite and swallowing. "We talked about the murders. All of them. Can you believe he and Peterson *still* think Kyle killed Carolee, Sam, and Emma . . . which doesn't give me too much faith in New York's Finest. I yelled at them about that. Then we talked about Jan. They pointed out that Jan's a freshman. According to common sense, and his records, he was away at some prep school when Carolee and Sam were killed, so that would rule out his being their murderer. Which means he might be a copycat. We tried to figure out if he was strong enough to have held me down like that in the bathroom—or to break the door of the suite. Peterson thinks he *could* have. He says some guys can be skinny dweebs one minute and monsters the next. But I doubt it, and so does Russo. Russo chased my attacker for a couple of blocks before losing him. He said the guy was fast . . . and built. Which doesn't sound at all like Jan. So, assuming the guy who attacked me was the same guy who killed Lauren—"

"It could have been someone else," Julie said.

"Right."

"Then who was it?" Julie asked.

Kirsten shook her head. The whole thing was so confusing. The closer they got, the further they seemed from an answer. Was there someone else who wanted to hurt Kirsten? Someone they hadn't even thought of?

The chirping sound of Outkast's "Hey Ya!", as played by cell phone, interrupted the conversation. Kirsten made a mental note to change that. It was embarrassing. "Hello?" she said, answering the phone.

There was a pause at the other end. And then a voice said, "Kirsten? Is this Kirsten Sawyer?" The voice was muffled and distorted—a hugely bad cell phone connection.

"You have to speak up," Kirsten said. "Who is this?"

"Kirsten," the voice said, "you don't know me. My name is Rich Stone."

Kirsten swallowed hard. Julie, noticing the change in Kirsten's face, dropped her burger and was staring intently across the table.

"S-Stone?" Kirsten repeated, her pulse quickening. "As in—"

"I'm Paul's brother," the voice interrupted. "*Kyle's* brother. I need to talk to you. It's a matter of life and death."

18

"Is this some kind of sick joke?" Kirsten whispered into the phone, her voice dry and parched. "How do I know you're Kyle's brother?"

Julie's jaw dropped. "Kyle's brother?" she whispered. "How could he have a brother without you knowing?"

Kirsten held up her index finger to her mouth, shushing her. She leaned against the window, trying to blot out the clank and clatter of the restaurant.

"It's not a joke," the voice answered. "I have to speak to you. Didn't he tell you about me? Didn't he talk about his eccentric but loving family?"

It was a familiar voice. Something about the words, the rhythm, something she couldn't put her finger on. She couldn't tell if he sounded like Kyle—the way brothers' voices are sometimes similar—because the connection was so bad. "I'm going to hang up," Kirsten said.

"No! Please don't. Kyle *must* have told you things about himself. Ask me anything about him. Test me. I'll prove we're related."

Her mind reached back. Did Kyle mention a brother? He did tell her *some* things about his family and himself—on a night that seemed like ages ago, in a dingy little room on the Upper West Side, near Columbia, where they lay awake until sunrise, talking—back before she'd found out his real identity. He was a great storyteller, making her laugh about funny incidents during his childhood. . . .

"He had a nickname . . . as a boy," Kirsten said, remembering one vivid, painful little description.

"TP," the muffled voice shot back.

Kirsten swallowed. *Yes. He's right.* "Why was he called that?" she pressed on.

"Because when he was in kindergarten, our mom thought it would be cute to dress him up as 'Prince Charming' for Halloween. So she put him in a costume that looked like a roll of toilet paper and gave him a crown and a toilet-paper cape. And for about three years, kids called him TP. He *hated* that!"

That was true too. Kyle had described the embarrassing incident during the one night they'd spent together and Kirsten had laughed and laughed.

"Where are you?" Kirsten demanded.

"I'm walking . . . somewhere in Central Park. Where no one can hear me. Where there are places to hide. I can't let myself be seen. He's after me now, the person who killed Sam . . . and my brother."

"You know who the killer is?" Kirsten's heart felt like a jackhammer. "Tell me!"

"Look, it's not the red-haired guy, and definitely not the kid who was your roommate—"

"How do you know about them?" Kirsten asked.

"It's someone else, and I'm determined to nail him. I have some new information that needs investigating. All along I've been *trying* to find this monster without dragging you in. But everything has changed, Kirsten. For one thing, he's on to me. I'm not sure how, but he knows I'm closing in. So I can't act alone anymore. It's too dangerous. And now you're in danger too. The killer tried to get you last night. You and I need to band together. We have no one else. Believe me, I wouldn't ask you if it weren't absolutely necessary."

Kirsten blanched. He knew about what had happened this morning. That the killer had been after her, not Lauren. How? How did he know? And what "information" did he have? Could this be it—the break? Could this be the missing link for the whole case?

Chill, Kirsten, she told herself. *Don't trust anyone. Go slowly.* "What do you want me to do?" she asked tentatively.

"I want you to meet me," he answered. "Right now. I'll tell you everything."

Kirsten was breaking out in a sweat. "It has to be somewhere public, where there are a lot of people around."

"We can't do it, then. Too risky. I'll have to go it alone—"

"Wait," Kirsten said. "Where did you have in mind?"

"How fast can you get to Central Park— the East Ninety-sixth Street entrance?"

Central Park? Kirsten's hopes shriveled as she glanced out the window. The sun had set, and the black February night had spread over the city. The park would be empty and dark. "I'm not an idiot," she said. "No one in her right mind would agree to meet a stranger after dark in Central Park."

"Not *deep* inside the park. Near the sidewalk. The playground—you know, the one just inside Fifth and Ninety-sixth, up the little hill? It's close to the entrance. We'll meet near the playground gate. There will be a downhill slope to your back. Right down to Fifth Avenue. If you get cold feet, you're out of there in a shot. One yell, and a thousand people hear. Not that you'll need to run. Or yell. You will want to hear what I say, Kirsten."

"I don't know," Kirsten said, fighting back tears.

Julie was holding on to her arm, not saying anything, just being supportive. Somehow knowing that Kirsten needed exactly that.

"Look, you have to understand the risk *I'm* taking. I'm leaving myself open to *you*. You could bring a posse of friends with you. Or the police, for all I know." He sighed. "Think about it. And come alone. I'll wait ten minutes, in a place where I can see you coming. If you're not alone, I'm afraid the meeting is off. I'll be long gone."

"Ten minutes?" Kirsten looked at her watch: 6:03.

"I can't hang around in one place. I have to keep moving. So if I don't see you after ten minutes, I'll leave. No hard feelings. You'll never hear from me again. But I hope you'll give me a chance. For my brother's—"

The line went dead. No more juice. Stupid. She had forgotten to charge it this morning.

As Kirsten pulled the phone away from her ear, Julie nearly jumped out of her seat. "Are you going to tell me what the hell *that* was about?"

Kirsten slipped the phone into her purse, her mind exploding with confusion. Was it total lunacy to want to go? Was she being a fool? There had to be a way to do this right. Some way to do what he wanted and still protect herself.

Kirsten checked her watch: 6:04. Nine minutes. "Come on, Jules. I'll tell you on the way."

Kirsten didn't know how much cash she had left on the table at Jackson Hole. But it was probably enough to insure great service from that waiter forever.

As she led Julie toward the park, she told her the whole story. They arrived, breathless, at the Ninetieth Street entrance to the park, across from the Church of the Heavenly Rest—six blocks south of the playground. By that time, the details of Kirsten's plan had fallen into place.

"Okay, you make your way to the playground along the East Drive," Kirsten said, gesturing inside the park to the path that ran around the Reservoir. "Keep under the lights. Stay with the joggers."

"What joggers?" Julie said, peering into the deserted park.

Kirsten looked at her watch again. "Go fast, we only have three and a half minutes. I will run like hell up Fifth Avenue and enter the park where he's expecting me. You hang out in the trees along the path, just south of the playground—and make sure you can see me. If he doesn't seem legit, call 911. Ready?"

"I don't know if I'm—" Julie began.

"Go!" Kirsten whispered.

As Julie bounced reluctantly into the park,

Kirsten raced up the bumpy sidewalk along the Central Park wall. She nearly tripped over a homeless man sprawled on a park bench. Her lungs ached from lack of exercise; her brain screamed, *Go back. Get Julie. GO HOME!*

This was crazy, insane. But she fought back the doubts. She had to trust her instincts. She had to give this a shot or she'd never know for sure.

She reached Ninety-sixth Street at 6:14.

A minute over.

He'd be history by now. That was what he'd said.

She scanned the area for anyone leaving the park. A bus trundled out of the transverse drive at Ninety-sixth, but that was it. No other person in sight. She turned toward the pedestrian gate in the stone wall.

As she entered the park and walked toward the playground, it was as if someone had thrown a sudden blanket over the sounds of the city. Her footsteps echoed dully in the hush, and a sharp westerly wind blasted her face. She drew the collar of her sailor coat tighter and headed off the path toward the playground gate to her left. The East Drive's distant streetlamps silhouetted the play equipment, making it look like a collection of hulking dinosaur skeletons.

Kirsten stepped inside the Cyclone fence gate, which she expected would have been locked by now. She couldn't see much in the darkness, but an orange pinpoint of light suddenly moved to her left.

Kirsten's breath caught. She moved closer. A wisp of smoke rose from the orange dot. It was a cigarette, moving up and down as a person took a drag.

A man. Dressed in a bulky, hooded down coat.

She turned and squinted into the distant blackness beyond the fence. Another figure was moving stealthily among the bushes, and she trusted it was Julie. Julie would be here by now.

Kirsten turned back to the man and opened her mouth to speak, but nothing came out. *Calm down*, she commanded herself. "Rich?" she squeaked.

When the guy didn't answer, she tried again, louder. "Are you Rich?"

"Not by Upper East Side standards," came the reply, "but comfortable."

The face inside the hood smiled at Kirsten. He was old—*grandfatherly*—and from nearby came a wheezy little pug that had just peed against a swing set. "Well, Stetson, shall we?" the man said to the dog. He stood up, nodded at Kirsten, and led the dog out of the playground.

As Kirsten watched them go, her spirits sank.

Kyle's brother was gone.

She'd blown it.

"We blew it!" she called out in the direction of the shadow she hoped was Julie. Kicking a rock against the fence, she began heading back toward Fifth Avenue.

And a dark figure leaped out of a shadow from behind a park bench.

"Who are you talking to?"

Kirsten gasped, jumping back. "Christ!"

"Sorry, didn't mean to scare you—who were you talking to?" The voice was whispered and muffled, just like it had been over the phone. The guy was wearing a black, full-face ski mask over his face.

"M-m-myself," Kirsten said. "I do that a lot. Who are you, anyway—and you'd better give me the answer I'm expecting or I'll scream so loud, the whole neighborhood will hear."

"Richard Stone," the guy said softly, stepping closer.

Kirsten backed away. He was between her and the gate now. She hoped he couldn't tell she was trembling. Her eyes flitted to the right. She also hoped Julie was calling the cops.

"Kirsten, you need to trust me," the guy said.

Stall him.

"Oh? Do you make a habit of jumping out of shadows wearing a ski mask?" she asked. "If you need to talk to me—if you're really who you say you are—*take off the mask.*"

"Fine," he said, slowly raising his hands toward his neck. Toward the bottom of the mask. "But you have to promise to hear me out. Deal?"

"Deal," Kirsten agreed.

Angling himself into the dim light of a distant streetlamp, he peeled off the mask.

Kirsten staggered back when she caught the first glimpse of his face. "It's, it's . . . you!" she cried.

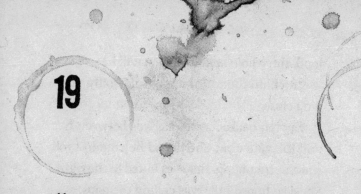

19

"You . . . ," Kirsten repeated.

The bony face . . . the narrow eyes . . . the smirk . . .

How had *Jan* managed to disguise his voice like that? How had he managed to fool her—*again?*

This was getting old. Very old.

"Sorry," Jan said. "Let me explain . . ."

Not this time, Kirsten thought. She shouted into the nearby bushes, *"Julie, call the cops!"*

Jan turned to look.

And Kirsten kicked him. Right where he lived.

He doubled over, groaning in agony. "Urrggh . . ."

Kirsten ran from the playground, around the Cyclone fence. Julie wasn't anywhere near the bushes, where she was supposed to be. She was standing in the middle of the East Drive. "Did you call the cops?" Kirsten shouted.

"There was a family of *rats* in the bushes!" Julie said. "I dropped the phone in there!"

"It was Jan, Julie. He was pretending to be Kyle's brother!"

"Oh, shit. What now?" Julie asked.

Kirsten looked over her shoulder. Jan had left the playground but was still inside the park, retching against the old stone wall. "My phone's dead, but there's a pay phone on the corner."

At the sound of distant footsteps, Julie looked over her shoulder. A jogger, all bundled up in a thick outfit and knit hat, appeared from around the downtown bend of the East Drive. "Go, Kirsten. I'll flag this guy down for help!"

Kirsten took off down the path toward the exit. But Jan was closer. He stumbled into the opening, his eyes red and angry. "We had a deal. You were going to hear me out."

"Get out of my way!" Kirsten shouted.

"Don't, Kirsten," Jan said. "Listen to me, please. I *am* Rich Stone."

He was crazy. Deluded.

She lunged for the exit and tried to push him, but he grabbed her arm. He was strong. Much stronger than he looked. As strong as her attacker in the Yellow Trance.

177

He was the one!

"HELP!" she shouted. *"HELLLP ME!"*

Jan pulled her into the shadows, holding her tight with one hand and putting his other hand over her mouth. He yanked her around so they were face-to-face.

Against the night-blackened bricks of the wall, his eyes seemed to float in a dark, featureless oval. "I tried to tell you," he rasped. "In the Party Room. I made a stupid mistake trying to be your roommate. I didn't want you to know then who I was, but I was wrong. I had to get you alone, where no one could hear us talk. I have something for you. Something you're not expecting . . ." Jan let go of her mouth and quickly pulled a small, dark object from his pocket.

Then his body stiffened, his eyes suddenly rising toward something over Kirsten's shoulder. "Oh, my God," he muttered. "Watch out, Kirsten! Duck!"

Kirsten felt herself being shoved, hard, to the side. She landed in the grass on her hand, crying out in pain. Charging down the path was the jogger Julie had seen. But Kirsten's eyes went right to the pistol in his hand—pointed at Jan!

Jan reared back and threw something. The black object hurtled through the air and connected with the jogger's face.

"Owwwwwww!" he screamed, and immediately Kirsten recognized the voice.

It was Russo! What was *he* doing here?

He stopped in his tracks, briefly, shaking his head with the shock. Julie was over the wall and Kirsten saw the top of Jan's hat racing down Fifth.

She scrambled to sit up, grimacing. Her hand was killing her.

Russo was moving again, through the exit, running after Jan. And Julie's arms were pulling her up. "Kirsten! Are you okay? Oh God, this was a dumb idea. I can't believe we came here. We could have been killed!"

Kirsten stared over the top of the wall, at the figure moving down Fifth Avenue. "That jogger was a cop," she said. "Sergeant Russo."

"The guy who was Jones?"

"Yes!"

"Jogging in the park with a gun? Does that make sense?"

"Nothing makes sense, Julie!"

"Well, it's a good thing he had a gun. Jan

was about to shoot you, Kirsten."

"No, he wasn't." Kirsten went over to the place where Jan had thrown the black object. It lay on the Central Park grass, a solid black rectangle against the darkness. She crouched and picked it up. "He was holding a PDA. An old one. He said he wanted to show it to me."

"Turn it on," Julie urged her. "What does it say?"

"The screen is cracked," Kirsten said. "It's useless."

At the sound of heavy breathing, they both jumped to their feet. Russo was heading back into the park at a jog. "Lost him," he grumbled as he came through the entrance, rubbing the bridge of his nose, which looked red and swollen. "Are you okay?"

Julie handed him the PDA. "Are you?"

"Only my plastic surgeon knows for sure," Russo replied, taking the device and fiddling with the controls. "Guess two things got busted. My nose and this."

"Do you always go jogging at night?" Kirsten asked.

"I'm just keeping an eye on you," Russo replied. "Lost track of you at Jackson Hole, when I got distracted by my phone. You must have left in a big rush. Thought I saw you heading for the park but I wasn't sure, so I went to check it out, looked over the wall, and saw Julie all by herself. I ran in as fast as I could." He shrugged. "I never was very good at track and field. Did he hurt you?"

"I have another hand," Kirsten said, massaging the injured one. "You know what he told me? That he was Kyle's brother! Can you believe that? He was so strong. He could have been the guy at Yellow Trance. And he's clearly out of his mind. I know you guys don't think so, *but he might be the one!*"

Russo exhaled, shoving the PDA into his pocket. "I'll show this to our IT guy. And I guess we'll be digging into the deVries records again. Come on, I'll drive you girls home."

"Wait," Julie blurted out as Kirsten and Russo began heading out of the park. "Did any of you notice what he *did?* Kirsten, he *pushed you aside* when Sergeant Russo came running with a gun. He yelled '*watch out.*' He was trying to protect you. What kind of killer does that?"

Julie was right. He'd told her to duck. If he'd been a murderer, he'd have held on to her. Put her in the line of fire.

Russo gave Julie a crooked, admiring smile. "Good question," he said.

Kirsten slouched out of the elevator and into her bedroom before her parents had a chance to see the grass stains on her clothes and the new blood flowing on her bandage. Then she quickly sneaked into the bathroom for a long soak in the Jacuzzi and a re-acquaintance with her delicious H_2O body lotion. Nothing like the scent of the sea to clear the brain and soothe an aching hand.

The ride home had been short, Julie and Kirsten staying silent while Russo called in a report to the precinct. From the sound of the conversation, Peterson was every bit as confused as they were.

Who was Jan? Was he the killer? A few minutes ago, she'd been convinced.

But he tried to save you. He put himself in the possible path of a bullet.

It now didn't seem possible he was a murderer.

He was trying to show her something. Maybe there was a clue on the PDA.

Maybe he really *was* Kyle's brother. . . .

She imagined the two faces, side by side in her mind. She'd never thought about it before, but there *was* a resemblance. Sort of. If you sharpened all of Kyle's angles, curled his hair, scrunched his features up.

She thought and thought until she started falling asleep, and then hauled herself out of the tub, lotioned up, and dressed for bed.

"Good night," she called out to her parents as she slipped into her room.

"'Night, sweetie," her mom said, peeking inside. "Everything okay? Nice dinner with Julie?"

"Totally fine," Kirsten lied.

"Well, tomorrow's a big day. Your new apartment is waiting. Daddy's friend Ed the real estate man made sure you got a nice view."

Kirsten nodded and forced a smile. Out of the corner of her eye she noticed her computer monitor still glowed with a screen saver slide show of the beach at Mykonos. When her mom left, she jumped up, went to her desk, and grabbed the mouse. The screen saver gave way to a million dead IMs and her Outlook Express program.

As she prepared to close down, she saw the latest e-mail message on her NYU account.

It was from JDVRIES.

What did he want? Where was he?

Shaking, she scrolled to the message. It was an image—a black-and-white newspaper clipping. The headline was "Alleged Portland-Area Teenage Murderer Paul Stone Buried; Parents Claim Innocence to End."

In the center of the photo, a casket was being lowered into the ground. The hole was surrounded by friends and family members dressed in black. Three figures were holding one another, as if for dear life—a thin man with a deeply lined face, a tall woman with an old-fashioned veil, and a young man in a jacket that seemed two sizes too large. Despite the photo's graininess, there was no mistaking the tears streaking the boy's beaklike nose and bony cheeks. There was no mistaking the face, either.

"Oh, God," Kirsten murmured. "It's Jan." She leaned closer, her chest pounding, and read the tiny caption underneath the photo:

Family members of the alleged murderer grieve (l to r): father Kirk Stone, mother

Elizabeth, brother Richard.

Below the image was a message:

KS—

I hope you're OK.

Please be OK.

don't know who that guy was in the park today. don't know if he was the killer or not.

I do know he followed me, but didn't get a good look at him.

I tried to get you out of harm's way. I hope I did.

As you can see by this picture, I wasn't lying. I am Richard Stone.

I'm not giving up on you. If you can, pls meet me tmw. I will wait. 6 a.m. 12th Ave. & 132nd, in the Fairway Parking lot. I wish it could be someplace nicer, but I don't want anyone to see me. I wish I could make you believe me. I wish I could be sure that you wouldn't try

185

to arrest me or get me in worse trouble than I already am.

I wish, I wish, I wish.

Kirsten, I am so in trouble.

I'll be waiting.

Be alone.

I mean it.

—RS

20

"You're meeting him?"

Julie's voice came over the cell as the taxi turned under the elevated highway near 125th Street.

They were stuck at a red light. Ahead of them, enormous vaulted steel columns rose above a decrepit road lined with metal-gated auto body shops and food distributors. Kirsten felt in her shoulder bag for the envelope with Kyle's picture, which she'd tucked snugly into the bottom. And the printout she'd made of the newspaper clipping Jan had e-mailed.

She quickly told Julie all about the note from Jan.

"So he was telling the truth. Great, Kirsten. Still, that doesn't mean you should meet him alone."

"I'll be fine," Kirsten said.

"But you never know," Julie pleaded. "This

guy is unpredictable and strange. You don't really know much about him. You said Kyle thought he was being framed. What if this kid turns out to be Kyle's psycho brother who did it all and then killed Kyle to get back at his parents who didn't love him enough? And now he's come to take possession of the only woman his brother ever truly loved."

"Julie!" Kirsten cried.

"Okay, so it's totally far-fetched, but it *is* possible—right?" Julie replied. "I mean, no one else could have known so much about Kyle: his girlfriends, his hangouts, his schedule—"

"But he was Paul's *brother.*"

"Cain was Abel's brother!" Julie said, taking a deep breath. "Sorry. I didn't mean that. Anyway, you should at least let people know where you are. Like me. Just in case."

"Gotta go," Kirsten said as the taxi turned left alongside the hulking orange-painted Fairway Market building.

As she pressed Off, Julie's words echoed in her mind. The theory wasn't very likely, but maybe Kirsten *was* being too trusting.

She glanced at the printout of Jan's

photo—at his devastated face at the funeral. A murderer would not look like that at the funeral of someone he had killed. Julie was being overly cautious.

Oh well, that's what friends are for.

Still, Kirsten felt a little funny as the cab headed toward the Hudson River. The water was whitecapped and silvery in the morning sun. It looked like miles to New Jersey on the other shore. The current was strong. Incredibly strong.

Anything dropped into that river would be swept away, never to be found again. Like, say, a body—if there *was* a hypothetical killer lurking around.

Easy, Kirsten. It's just a meeting.

Still. Julie was right about one thing: Better to be safe than sorry. Someone *should* know where she was. She whipped out her cell as the cab stopped at the Stop sign at Twelfth Avenue, near the front of the market. To her right was the now-empty display of fruits and veggies all covered with canvas, tended by a lone worker in khakis and a woolen watch cap. Just across the street, the parking lot's entrance was blocked by a chain-link fence with a blue-and-orange Closed sign.

Where is he? Kirsten wondered.

"What now?" the driver asked.

"I—I don't know," Kirsten said as she tapped out Julie's number.

Was Jan supposed to find me, or vice versa?

From the dashboard of the cab, a voice crackled over the intercom: "Police alert, Harlem area—car 3029, do you read me?"

As the driver picked up his intercom to answer, the passenger door to the right opened. The man in khakis slipped into the seat next to her, taking her wrist. "Please don't. You don't need to call anyone. I'm really glad you're here."

He wasn't a Fairway worker.

He was Jan!

"H-Hi," Kirsten stammered, turning off the cell.

"Go left," Jan said to the driver, his eyes intense, wary, darting every which way.

He wasn't looking Kirsten in the face at all.

This did not make her feel comfortable.

"Listen buddy, I already have a passenger," the cab driver said, covering up his intercom.

"We're friends," Jan replied. "Didn't she tell

you she was meeting someone?"

In the rearview mirror, Kirsten could see the driver's probing eyes staring back. Trying to gauge if this unexpected intrusion was okay.

She didn't know how to respond. *Was* it okay? She wasn't sure anymore. Smiling back noncommittally, she put her cell phone away.

The driver muttered something to the person at the other end of the intercom, then turned down Twelfth Avenue.

"Did you call someone?" Jan asked.

"No," Kirsten said.

"But you were about to."

"Well, I didn't see you. I got nervous."

Jan nodded and took a deep breath. His forehead was beaded with sweat, his eyes bloodshot. "So . . . no one followed you?"

"No, Jan. No. We're alone. What's this all about?"

"I don't usually operate like this," he replied, his voice tense. "I feel like we're in some kind of film noir." As they reached the next corner, he leaned closer to the driver. "Go left again, and then left under the elevated highway."

"Where are we going?" Kirsten asked, looking at the grimy, boarded-up storefronts.

"Where are you taking me?"

"Two blocks up," Jan said to the driver. "On the right—the Happy Morning coffeeshop."

It was a small, dingy place with two other yellow taxis parked in front. Jan shoved a few dollar bills on the front seat and hurried out of the cab.

"I'll sit at the empty table," Jan said softly as Kirsten got out. "You order for us at the counter and act totally normal. I'll have a black coffee and glazed doughnut, please, and order whatever you want. My treat. It's the least I can do."

"Thanks," Kirsten said uncertainly.

The empty table happened to be the *only* table inside. The other customers—mostly men in drab uniforms—sat silently at a counter over coffee, pastries, and the *Daily News.*

Kirsten ordered the breakfast from a dour woman with hair that looked as if it hadn't seen shampoo since New Year's Day. As Kirsten walked back to the table, Jan sat staring intently out the window, shaking his right leg.

"I'm so glad you're all right," he said, not sounding too glad about anything. "I was worried that the guy in the park would hurt you. Did you manage to get the PDA?"

Kirsten shook her head. "It's dead. The screen cracked."

"Oh, great," Jan said, looking away in disgust. "Paul kept a journal on his computer at home. I spent a month trying to crack his password—and I transferred the whole damn thing to my PDA. I wished you'd read it. He was a really gifted writer, you know. Did you know that? Did he ever tell you that?"

"Um, no," Kirsten said.

"Well, he was. He wanted to be a novelist— would have been a great one too. But he couldn't write anything too personal, anything that might tip people off. We were all living under fake names. We had to. After Paul's arrest, the whole family was disgraced. Paul lost his admission to Brown, Dad lost his job, Mom was being eased out of hers. We moved to North Dogsquat, Massachusetts, and became another family—legal name-change. Me, the family IT genius, I figure out how to alter records, make a past disappear and a new one emerge. Paul couldn't stand it. All his life he'd been, like, Mr. Confessional Suffering Writer-Poet, and now he couldn't even be Paul Stone. So Mom pulls a few strings, gets him into Bowdoin—and in the middle of his freshman year, some smart-ass kids catch on. They start calling him 'Paul' to see if he turns around. . . . He can't take it . . . but he does. . . ." Jan's voice trailed off.

Something was up. His speech was rapid, high-pitched. His fingers were tapping the edge of the table, his eyes constantly moving.

Kirsten swallowed uncomfortably. *Uppers,* she thought. *Big-time.* "Um, was this why you brought me here?" she asked.

Jan pinned her with his glance. "No! Am I boring you?"

Whoa. She eyed the door. Jan was positioned between it and her—right by the handle.

"I worshipped him, do you understand?" Jan said. "He told me *I* was the family genius—the next Tarantino, the Great American Filmmaker. And I'm, like, yeah right—we're hiding from the world in disgrace, and I'm supposed to make films? So I quit. Gave up. Took a job in a video store. I think it broke his heart to see that. I think that's the reason he came to New York. Not for his own sake. For *mine.* For his family. To clear our names. That's the kind of guy he was, *do you understand?*"

Kirsten nodded. He was freaking out right in front of her. She sat forward, at the edge of her seat, planting her toes firmly.

"On the day he died, I decided I *would* make that film," Jan went on. "But not what he would have expected—some postmodern, nihilistic shoot-'em-up, *Kill Bill Seventeen.* Hell, no. A documentary—the biggest exposé of all time. The East Side Murders, *solved.* Collect the facts, let them speak for themselves—not only art, but truth! Cinema-verité. The audience tastes the blood, feels the agony of death and then, *wham,* the primal shocker when the murderer is revealed. *In Cold Blood* meets *Titicut Follies. . . .*"

Kirsten hadn't the slightest idea what he was talking about.

He was on a roll. With himself.

He needed help. Professional help.

Go. Now. Kirsten sprang for the door.

His hand was like a lash, holding the door firmly shut. "Sorry. Sorry. I'm scaring you. I'm rambling. Sit. We're partners, Kirsten."

"No fighting about the check, lovebirds." The haggard-looking woman swooped across the floor, plopping the plates down on the table. "Out of muffins. Rye toast is on the house."

As she went away, Jan reached into his jacket pocket. He pulled out a thick envelope and spilled the contents on the table. "Recognize any of these?" he asked.

On the top was the newspaper clipping from Kyle's burial. Kirsten held it up. It had yellowed, and had ads on the reverse side. A real clipping. Nothing fake or Photoshop-ed.

She set it down. Underneath were all kinds of photos. A young Kyle in a jacket and Talcott tie, on his first day of school, arm in arm with his brother . . . Kyle and Jan, both much younger, under a Christmas tree, tearing open presents . . . an older and sadder-looking Kyle—the Kyle *she* knew—in a short-sleeved shirt on a snowy college campus . . .

"Bowdoin," she said.

Jan nodded. He fished around and pulled out another image—Kyle with four friends. "Recognize these guys? Their names were Moyer, Goldstein, Willett, and Schloss."

The sounds of their names took her breath away. Of course she knew who they were. She would never forget those names, never forget

the awful story Kyle had confided. . . .
"They're Kyle's b-ball bros from Talcott," she
said. "The guys who were with him on the
night when . . .

"When everything started going wrong,"
Jan said. "When they all got juiced and got in
a car and ran down some cute little public-
school girl—"

"Gina," Kirsten said. "That was her
name."

"They were tanked that night," Jan said.
"All of them. My brother, too. Plus, he was
upset about his girlfriend, Carolee, who was
hooking up with some other guy. But he didn't
do anything to Gina! It was the other guys!"

"I know. And then that same night—"
Kirsten began.

"Carolee . . . ," Jan said, nodding.

"Dead too," Kirsten added. "Beaten. Hands
bound with a Talcott tie. His tie. He had left it
in some bar—the Zoo. Someone must have
taken it."

"He was eaten up by that," Jan said. "By
the idea that he should have come forward
about Gina—that he should have pushed
harder about his own innocence. The whole

thing broke him. He didn't deserve it."

Jan's face was swollen and sad, and he wiped a tear. He turned away, too embarrassed to face her but too hurt to not let it show. It reminded her of the look on Kyle's face when he'd told her the story—and she reached out to Jan across the table. "I know how you feel."

"I loved my brother," Jan said softly.

"I did too," she replied, and leaned over to give him a hug. They sank into each other's arms for a moment, comforting, remembering the one person they missed *so much*, and before Kirsten pulled away, she closed her eyes and pictured him—pictured Kyle with his strong frame and his handsome face and beautiful wavy dark hair. As long as she kept her eyes shut, she could *imagine*, she could blot out the last year and imagine what could have happened between them, what their lives together might have been like. But just as fleeting as Kyle's image came to her, it disappeared. It was time for Kirsten to open her eyes and face reality.

"Tell me," she said. "Tell me why you brought me here."

Jan buried his face in his hands. "I—I'm feeling really messed up, Kirsten. You know? There's so much more I want to say, but I have to know . . . do you believe me?"

"I do," Kirsten said. She glanced out the window at the yellow cabs parked outside. If she needed a ride home, all she'd have to do was raise her hand in the coffeeshop and three guys would fall all over one another for the fare.

But she had to give him something first.

The photo.

He was the brother. That was certain. No matter what he'd done, he was the brother. And he deserved the picture as much as she did.

She pulled the envelope from her pack. "Jan—I mean, Richard? I took this from your brother's hands after he died. No one but me has seen it."

Jan's eyes widened as he gently took the photo, his face growing pale at the sight of his brother and Carolee, tanned and smiling. "They used to hang at this place all the time. Must have been just before . . ."

"Keep it," Kirsten said. "Maybe you can use it for your film."

Screeeeeeeee! Tires squealed outside the

coffeeshop as two cop cars skidded to a stop.

Jan turned, shoving the photo in his pocket.

The front door flew open. Customers hit the floor as Russo raced in, gun drawn and grabbed Jan by the back of his collar. "What the—?" Jan blurted out. "What do you think you're doing?"

"Sergeant Russo, stop!" Kirsten pleaded. "He hasn't done anything!"

But a swarm of blue uniforms barged into the room, blocking Kirsten—and she could only watch helplessly as another officer escorted Jan outside, muttering, "You have the right to remain silent, anything you say can be used against you in a court of law . . ."

"Don't mean to scare you, Kirsten," Russo said. "But when the call came in from the cab driver, we jumped. We've been looking for you—and him—all morning. Peterson just got an item from an identity-tracking company. This guy is not who he says he is."

"I know he isn't! He's—"

But Russo had slapped the copy of a passport photo on the table.

Jan's face.

"You set me up!" Jan's hysterical voice shouted over the din. *"Kirsten—you set me up!"*

Kirsten looked closer. Under the smiling face was a name.

FRANK HARMON.

A name she had never heard in her life.

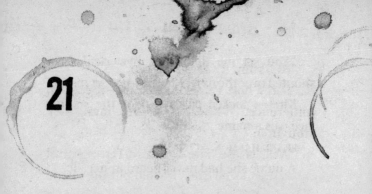

21

As she passed under the Washington Square Arch later that morning, Kirsten tried the precinct again for what seemed like the hundredth time.

It had been a horrible day. After the Happy Morning breakfast, she should have gone straight to her new apartment, but the thought of that depressed her, so she went to classes—and spent most of the time in tearful conversations about Lauren.

She missed Lauren. Lauren would have known what to make of this morning's total twisted bizarreness.

Frank Harmon?

Just when things seemed to be straightening out, *a whole new person.* It didn't make any sense!

"Eighty-eighth Precinct," answered the voice of Trudy, the dispatcher.

"Hi, Trudy, it's Kirsten again."

"Sorry, hon. Peterson and Russo are still in conference. With that young man they brought in."

"Well, please have Detective Peterson call me as soon as he can." Kirsten put the phone away as she walked into her new building on Lower Fifth Avenue. A team of men in uniforms greeted her by name, and she rode up silently in the elevator with people who looked like their faces had been carved from granite.

She was the only one left when she got out on the penthouse floor.

Dad had proudly called her place a "furnished apartment" in "one of the finer art deco properties on Lower Fifth Avenue." Well, *furnished* was a loose term. She felt like she'd walked onto the set of *Six Feet Under.* The curtains were made of a dark maroon velvet brocade, hanging over the windows in heavy swooshes that blocked any hint of light. The carpet looked like the lifelong project of some poor Turkish slaves who had poured their blood and guts into it. Literally. And the gaudy, over-sized chandelier brought back unpleasant memories of sitting through *The Phantom of the*

Opera with her fifth-grade class while Herman Finkel kept trying to feel her left breast.

She half expected to find the previous owner still there, gray and forgotten and covered with dust in the closet. *Don't mind me, dear. . . .*

Dad's movers had done it all: fixed up her bedroom, made her bed, put towels on the bathroom rack, arranged her furniture. They'd even brought along a techie to set up her cable TV, desktop computer, scanner, and a wireless network for her laptop. They left her personal stuff in boxes—thank God—but she was too tired to deal with that.

She was too tired to do anything.

She collapsed onto her bed. Her laptop had been turned on and set on a swivel-table built into the wall. She swung it around, hit the touch pad to get rid of the screen saver, and found that it had been set to the home page of founder/co-owner Edward P. Spencer of Cloverdale Realtors, "For All Your High-End Needs."

Cute.

Julie had sent an IM—'SUP? WHERE R U?—and she was still online.

Kirsten typed COME OVER NOW, 9 5TH AVE. U WONT BELIEVE THIS PLACE! and pressed send, when her cell phone rang. She glanced at the screen—Peterson's number!—and picked up the call.

"Where is he?" Kirsten blurted out. "What happened, Detective Peterson?"

"Russo here," Russo's voice came back to her. "Your friend Peterson is a little embarrassed. Well, no, *a lot*. See, it turns out that your pal Jan is not only Frank Harmon, but also Bill Riddly, Otis Saunders, Quincy Fielding, Barney Snipp . . . and a few others."

Kirsten sank into her pillow. "What does *that* mean?"

"Some people build model airplanes for a hobby," Russo said with a sigh, "Jan builds fake identities. On the Web. Posts them so they can be picked up by the information-harvesting services. Just made-up names. He thinks it's fun. Says he first learned the art of it when his family *really* had to change their names, and he got hooked. Jan deVries—that was the most detailed fake he created. Fooled NYU."

And you, Kirsten chose not to say. "But who *is* he, then?" she asked.

"Stone. Richard Stone. We're one hundred percent positive now. We've got corroboration from childhood doctors, a faxed birth certificate from the hospital, the works. It's iron-clad, Kirsten."

Kirsten breathed a sigh of relief. He was legit. He *was* Kyle's brother. She began to laugh. "Barney Snipp?"

"That was my favorite too. Anyway, he gave me a lecture. Said I could have done better than the name 'Jones.' Jones was boring." Russo chuckled. "Wise guy."

"Can I speak to him?" Kirsten asked.

"We let him go," Russo said.

"To where?"

"I don't know. He's free. We couldn't keep him here. My guess is, he's sleeping. Between you and me, I think he was a little high this morning. But I wouldn't worry about him, Kirsten. He's not the guy who killed your roommate . . . or any of the others. Or the guy who attacked you at the Yellow Trance. With any luck, he'll help us find the real murderer. He had some pictures with him and says he may have some more."

Kirsten gulped. He had photos all right. Like the one she'd given him. The one she'd stolen from Kyle's body. If Russo knew about that one, he wasn't saying.

"Do you have any leads?" she asked hopefully. "On Kyle's killer?"

"At the moment," Russo replied with a big sigh, "no."

"This is my krend Fiercesten," Julie said, dancing over to the bar of the trendy new Karib Club with her usual five guys in tow. "I mean, fend Krirsten. I mean, I'm too loaded right now, so talk amongst yourselves . . . anything else is extra credit. Woo-hoo!"

She whirled away with three of the boys, leaving two with Kirsten. One had a Cheshire cat grin and a swoop of hair in front that reminded her of the Kennedy Airport terminal. The other, Kirsten had to admit, was crush material—tall, shy smile, blue eyes, soft features, a total Prince William type, only hotter. "I'm sorry, how did you pronounce that name?" he asked in a sexy British accent that nailed the image.

"Any way she wants to," Hair Swoop said. "I'm George Brent, and this is Charles Mansfield, my roommate."

"I'm Kirsten." She gave them a flip of her hair and a slow once-over. She was trying to get into the mood. She needed a break. But so much was on her mind. She hadn't heard a thing from Jan all day. Did he still think she'd set him up at the Happy Morning? He'd never had told her who he thought the killer was— and that was what scared her the most. For all she knew, he could be here. Tonight.

He could be one of these two guys that Julie had deposited.

Loosen up, Kirsten. It's been a long day. Kirsten turned to put her drink down. She lifted her arms and began to dance, moving her hips in rhythm, sending her chest in all kinds of directions followed closely by George's and Charles's radar eyes.

"Wooooo!" shouted George, whose energy did not quite make up for his lack of rhythm. Charles was more reserved, but hot, hot, hot, in an I'm-so-cool-I-don't-like-to-show-off way.

"Are the girls in England like this?" Kirsten asked Charles.

"Wales," he said with a smile.

DZZZZZ. Her cell phone vibrated against her thigh, and she snatched it up, poising her finger over the Off button. She didn't recognize the return number, but it was a 212 area code without a nametag. Kirsten tagged all her numbers. What *stranger* would be calling at this hour?

"Hello?" she said, lifting the phone to her ear as she danced.

"I know who did it," a familiar voice said.

Kirsten put her finger in her other ear to blot out noise. "Who is this? Hello?"

"It's Richard. And I said, *I know who did it.*"

"You *what?*" Kirsten blurted out.

"Shhhh. Sounds like you're in a public place. Meet me at the Eighty-sixth Street subway station at one forty-five."

Kirsten looked at her watch. It was almost 1:30. "You've got to be kidding. What did you find out? What happened to you today? You can't just tell me to come over there without an explanation!"

George and Charles had stopped dancing now and were looking at her with great concern and disappointment, like two fishermen watching a big catch that was about to get away.

"I'll be on the express platform, Kirsten," Richard said. "If you want to know who killed your best friend—and my brother—you will follow my instructions. Now."

Part Three

22

There she is.

She's leaving.

Now, MOVE, pal.

But do it right.

No boo-boos.

You blew it last time. TOTALLY BLEW IT!

Oh, that hurt.

She wasn't meant to die.

WHERE WAS YOUR CONTROL, BUDDY?

You could have looked. You could have turned on the light. SOMETHING.

That was a lapse. A very, very bad lapse.

But you can't dwell.

You can't live in the past.

Because let's face it, IT WASN'T YOUR FAULT.

Oh, no. If that bitch had come home the way she was supposed to . . . if she had been in her bed THE WAY SHE WAS SUPPOSED TO . . .

It would have turned out just dandy.

But she didn't. She went running to her rich Fifth Avenue mommy and daddy.

SHE SET HER ROOMMATE UP.

What kind of friend does that?

A pampered, coddled, morally bankrupt friend, that's who.

And because she set up her roommate, I missed my chance.

And because I missed my chance, she's alive.

And because she's alive, she's GETTING CLOSER.

Well, she did not play her cards right.

Because I'm calling in the chips.

Tonight's the night.

The girl has been living on borrowed time.

And when she goes, there will be none left. It will all stop.

Finally. All. Stop.

I'll miss it. Oh yes, I will. There has been some serious fun, along with the aggravation.

But when it's over, I will be able to rest again.

For the first time in years.

On your knees, little girl. Say a prayer.

And kiss your ass good-bye.

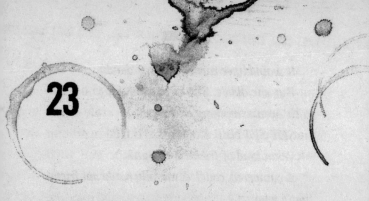

23

The headlights . . .

hurting her eyes . . . the streetlamps and the screaming halogen bulbs that flanked the entrances of Second Avenue apartment buildings . . . *Second Is Diving, Third Is Striving, Park Is Thriving, and Fifth Is Arriving.* Dad's old saying; what a crock. It was all so bright against the winter blackness and it made her dizzy, so Kirsten forced her footsteps one in front of the other, her mind a jumble of loose thoughts, her feet aching in her too-tight Jimmy Choos—and around the time she reached Eighty-Ninth Street, the mojitos seemed to kick in again and she was so tight, she could hardly see straight.

Focus, Kirsten . . .

She made a right at Eighty-sixth Street, passed the shuttered stores and the ragged, sleeping figures on the heating grates, and made a sharp left at Lexington Avenue to the subway entrance. She rushed down the stairs to get past the gentle updraft of stale urine that greeted her, and nearly tripped headlong into the puddle. At the turnstile she tried seven times to push her MetroCard through before realizing it was her driver's license.

Down past the empty local track . . . down another flight to the express level, where the Number 5 train was pulling out of the station. No one was left on the platform except the dark, rumpled heap of a homeless person against the distant tiles. She hated this station. It was long and narrow, and trains came from around a curve, so you never knew in advance.

But it had a bench. Thank God for benches. She slumped onto one and waited for the choppy waters in her mind to settle. As the train's sound receded into the tunnel, a soft crackling sound came up from the Dumpster at the end of the platform. She didn't want to think about what was scurrying around in the trash.

Her watch read 1:48. Jan . . . *Richard* should be here by now.

She closed her eyes—not a smart thing to do in the subway, but she didn't give a damn.

Shhhhp . . . shhhp . . . shhhp . . .

The sound was coming from her right. The homeless guy had risen and was shuffling toward her. His feet were wrapped in tattered plastic bags held together with masking tape.

Oh, great. She stood up from her seat and edged back toward the stairs.

"Hey, Kirsten." He was sprinting now.

No. This was not real. She was drunk and hearing things, and this guy could not possibly know her name. She turned to run, but the guy was on her, grabbing her arm!

"Oh no, you don't!" She forced her bleary eyes to focus into the shadow of the man's hood and recognized his face.

"It's me, Richard," he said.

"God, you scared me!" she shouted, her voice echoing down the tracks.

"Ssshhhh, we have to be quiet," he said.

"You *biter* not be laying . . . better not be lying—wait . . ."

"You're drunk, Kirsten."

"You don' look much better. You have a new *identity*, huh? Homeless Guy. Or do you have a name? Pleased to meet you. Barney Snipp, I presume?"

"This is bad. How can you help me if you're drunk?"

Hold steady. Look him in the eyes. All four of them. "How'm I supposed to help you? One minute you're a good guy and I like you, the next you're in disguise and doing something creepy—and tonight you called to say you know who did it and if you're playing with me, I'll—"

Richard gently put his finger on her lips. "Sshhh. Sober up, will you?"

"You jerk." Kirsten lurched forward, wanting to hurt him, somehow, but managed only to trip and fall into his arms.

He held her tightly. "I need you, Kirsten. My brother needs you. And we don't have much time. I know who the killer is."

"Who? Who did it, Richard? Tell me!"

Richard pulled open his ratty wool overcoat. A video camera hung from his neck. "There's an old saying in show business: 'Show, don't tell.' Tonight you and I are going to show the world who did it. We're going to expose him."

"A camera? You're making a film? *Now?*"

"We're both doing it. Me *and* you. Director and star. You're going to get the killer to confess, and I'm putting it on film. This is *it*, Kirsten. The big moment. And what a setting. The shabbiness, the urban grit, the rats on the tracks, the tunnel moving into darkness—*symbolism*—sex and death . . ."

She shook her head. This had to be a dream.

This wasn't a dream.

The man with a hundred identities . . . and it all boiled down to one: the same creep she'd seen for the first time in the Ridge lounge. Movie Geek from Hell.

He made her sick.

"Wait," she said. "Let me understand this. These are roles . . . you're *staging* this . . . you're playing a bag man, and I'm—"

"You're playing Kirsten, of course. Now, I need an establishing shot. So stand by the edge, looking uptown. I'll be sitting against the wall, looking pathetic." He pulled a manila envelope out of his coat and handed it to Kirsten. "When he comes down, show him what's in this envelope."

"Who?"

"The killer."

Kirsten's alcoholic haze lifted, as if slapped right out of her. This was worse than sick. "And who's playing that role?" she asked.

Richard exhaled hard. "Someone who you—"

The sound of footsteps on the stairs interrupted him.

"Here he comes," Richard said, then closed his jacket and ran back to his place against the wall. *"Just do what I told you to do!"*

Kirsten backed away. A guy stepped down from the stairs and walked onto the platform—young and bland-looking, in an Elvis-Costello-glasses-and-Converse-sneakers way. He gave Kirsten a quick once-over and looked up the tracks.

This was the killer? The actor playing the killer?

This was absurd. Grotesque. She didn't need to be sober to know that.

Still clutching the envelope, she backed toward the stairs—and she bolted.

Tripping on the stairs. Clutching the banister. Fighting the waves of nausea and drunkenness. The lights that seemed to whirl down from the ceiling and back up.

"Hey! You can't do this! Get back here!" Richard cried. He was moving fast. Much faster than she could.

Hang on. Hang on tight to the railing and move.

If she could get all the way up . . . to the transit clerk . . . she'd be safe.

Up . . . up . . .

Almost to the landing, when a hand landed heavily on her shoulder. "Stop!" Richard said.

"*Screw . . . you!*" Kirsten said. With all her strength, she leaned her weight into Richard and pushed.

"Aaaaaghh!" he screamed, windmilling his arms, falling. Falling down the subway steps.

Kirsten raced upward.

She made the lower landing, the one between the local and express. *Go. Keep going.*

Her feet were more steady now. She placed her head down and raced up to the main platform, through the turnstile, and sprinted for the exit. She could smell the air from outside, wafting down into the station.

She was almost there. Almost free.

And she ran smack into someone coming into the station.

"Oh!" she screamed.

"Whoa!" he said.

She stumbled backward. A tall, broad figure stepped out of a shadow.

Scott! Dressed in his usual basic black and looking like God.

"Kirsten?" he said with a slightly baffled smile. "What a coincidence."

"Oh, God," Kirsten said. "You have no idea how happy I am to see you."

She wanted to jump in his arms. She wanted to laugh and cry and kiss him and run away and go home to sleep, all of those things mixed up like a big, confusing emotional stew.

"Nice to see you, too. Is everything okay?" he asked.

"Fine! *Fine!*" Kirsten replied. Where are you going?"

"Home. Like I do every night."

"To Queens?"

"Brooklyn. But I just realized I have an errand to run for my little sister. Where are *you* going?"

"Home—to NYU!" Kirsten cried. This was

perfect. Scott could be her escort onto the train. Her bodyguard. Richard wouldn't *think* of messing with Scott. Not after the way Scott had treated him at the Party Room.

She almost blurted out what had just happened, but checked herself. She didn't want Scott to go after him. She didn't want a scene. Just a simple ride home. That would be enough. Well, maybe if Scott gave her an attractive alternative to going home, that would be worth a thought. . . .

"Looked like you were going in the other direction," Scott said.

"I got a little scared, that's all. You know. The subway at night? It's deserted."

Scott smiled. "Well, not anymore. Come on. Why waste twenty bucks on a cab ride?"

As he and Kirsten walked to the turnstile, she heard a rumble from below—another train trundling out of the station. A small group of passengers began emerging from the stairwell.

The "killer" was gone from the platform when they reached the bottom, but Richard was still there, hunched against the wall and looking like a poor, homeless person. His finest role. Kirsten almost laughed aloud, but she held her tongue. At the moment, Richard was probably shitting himself with fear at the sight of Scott.

At the end of the platform, Richard moved. Kirsten looked out of the corner of her eye. He was pointing the camera at them!

Incredible. He was going to film them.

She crossed her eyes at Richard and flipped him the finger.

Scott gave her a curious look and glanced over his shoulder. "That guy a friend of yours?"

Kirsten blushed. "Um . . . well, yeah. Actually he's not really homeless. He's a kid. A student. Trying to get some, um, interesting real-life experience—"

"As a bum?" Scott laughed. And that deep, rumbly, scrumptious laugh sounded three times as sexy echoing in the train tunnel. "I love college kids. Hey, is he taking *pictures* of us?"

Kirsten swallowed hard. "Just ignore him."

"Doesn't he know it's illegal to take pix in the subway these days?" Scott asked.

Kirsten could feel a gust of wind from the tunnel. Another train was approaching. Just in time. "How far down are you going?" she asked. "Is your errand before Astor Place?"

"Errand?" Scott said.

"The one for your little sister?" she replied.

Scott nodded. "Oh, right. As a matter of fact, that's at Astor Place too."

"Cool. I could . . . um, help you run it. The errand, I mean. And then, maybe you could show me Brooklyn. It's still early. Well, not really . . ." *Ugh. Be a little more obvious, why don't you, Kirsten?*

They pulled back from the edge, letting the Number 5 train roll in. As it screeched to a stop, she noticed that Richard had stood up. He was walking toward them.

Kirsten gave him a "go away" look, but he was moving faster now. His camera was down, and he was trying to say something, gesturing with his free hand. What was he *doing*?

Scott stood to the side of the door, motioning for Kirsten to enter the car. She rushed in, trying to keep his attention with a smile and a thank-you.

From halfway down the platform, Richard screamed, *"You didn't—"* But his voice was cut off by the electronic bell, the recorded "Stand clear of the closing doors" announcement, and the *whoosh* of the door.

"Don't I know that guy?" Scott asked.

Richard was standing outside the door, banging on it, holding up his camera. *"Open up!"* he shouted. *"Open the doors!"*

Kirsten hid her face in embarrassment. "Oh God, ignore him. He has been the biggest pain in my butt. He's crazy."

As the train pulled away, Richard began to run alongside it, keeping pace, pointing wildly at Kirsten.

"He's trying to tell you something," Scott said, plopping himself down on a seat. "What's that in your hand?"

Kirsten shrugged. "I don't know. He thinks he's Tarantino. He's trying to film a reenactment of the murders—and show them being solved, too. This was supposedly the climax— I was supposed to get the killer to confess. Some guy was down here, playing the murderer, but he disappeared. I had to give him this, but of course I didn't." Kirsten opened the envelope and slowly pulled out an eight-by-ten glossy photo.

She recognized it right away. It was a blow-up of Paul's photo, the one he'd been holding when he died. The one she'd given to Richard this morning. At this size, Paul's and Carolee's smiling faces seemed incandescent.

Along the bottom were the words DIGITALLY ENHANCED BY R. STONE. In the upper-right corner, a neon sign she hadn't noticed before now clearly read THE ZOO. Kirsten could recognize a couple of faces of people she knew somewhat, but not very well: Leslie Fenk's big sister, Ruthie . . . Paul's friend, Willets . . .

And someone else.

Someone she *did* know.

Someone she knew very well, but never, ever expected to see.

Scott tilted his head with a patient little smile. "Something juicy?" he asked.

She held the photo closer. To make sure.

The face was washed-out. Pixilated.

In the original photo it had been a dark blob, swallowed in the shadow of an overhanging bar-glass rack. But Richard had managed to bring out the features.

It was Scott.

Tending bar.

He had one arm on Paul's shoulder, another on Carolee's. Like old friends.

Old friends.

"Have a seat," Scott said, patting the place next to him. "Are you going to show me? What is it?"

"A picture. Kyle's in it," Kirsten said.

"That weird guy was a friend of Kyle's?"

"Um, yeah. I guess you could say that." Kirsten's mind was sharpening by the moment, and Scott's words from the night when they'd almost hooked up . . . from a conversation—a conversation about Kyle— were coming back to her,

"I'd never met him until he came in here that one time," Scott had said about Kyle. But it sure *looked* like he knew Kyle. Would he *forget* someone like that?

"Sentimental value," Kirsten said. "You wouldn't be interested. I mean, not unless you knew Kyle when this picture was taken. When he was a little younger. Back in the days when he was Paul Stone. You wouldn't have known him then, right?"

Scott shook his head. "Can't say I did."

"I mean, you *could* have known him, though—right? His hair was shaggier, and he was a little heavier. He went to Talcott Prep?

227

Hung out on the East Side? Dated a girl named Carolee Adams? You could have known him and forgotten?"

Scott laughed. "I have a photographic memory for customers. That's what makes me a good bartender. And, I assure you, I never met that dude. Or the girl."

But he had. Obviously, he had.

She could see it right in her hand. He knew Kyle and Carolee. He knew them when they were a couple. Before Carolee was murdered.

If he'd tended bar at the Zoo, he knew *all* of them. Paul and his buds hung there all the time. They had been there that awful night—the night they drove off . . . the night those guys . . . those idiots had killed that poor girl, Gina.

Paul had left his tie at the Zoo that night— the tie that had been used to kill Carolee only hours later. He'd left the tie on the bar. *Everyone knew that.*

Scott would have known it too. *So how could he say he didn't?*

Kirsten felt the blood rushing from her face. She slowly slipped the photo back into the envelope. The train, which had been moving fast, began to slow. The conductor announced construction delays, and out the window the tunnel's vertical beams passed like dried tree stumps from some burned-out world.

She needed time to think.

This wasn't right.

Scott was hiding something.

Why?

Was he hiding the killer's identity? Did he *know* who took the tie from the bar? Whoever the bartender was that night would know.

"Hey, are you feeling all right, Kirsten?" Scott asked.

He was going to be with her till Astor Place. It was a long ride from the Upper East Side. She had to say something. "Can you be honest with me, Scott? Did you tend bar at a place call the Zoo?"

Scott flinched. Just the tiniest shift of muscle across his right cheek. Kirsten could tell. She knew every inch of that face. "I think I did. Yes, I did. For a while . . . there have been so many bars."

"Then you know about the night of the Carolee Adams murder. I mean, even if you weren't there—even if you were, like, a sub— you would know about it, wouldn't you? The bartenders would have talked about that."

"I guess I do remember it. I—I block things out. Especially when I'm working double and triple shifts."

"Kyle told me he left a tie on the bar the night of Carolee's murder. *Did he?*"

Scott's eyebrow lowered across his forehead like a ledge. "She wasn't the only one murdered that day, Kirsten—remember? There was another girl."

Of course there was: Gina. But that was beside the point. Why was he bringing *that* up?

"Next stop will be Fifty-ninth Street," the recorded announcement chimed. They had a few more stops before they'd have to switch for the local. You needed the local for Astor Place. Astor Place would be kind of dead at this hour. It was a good thing she'd have company. How lucky for her that he had to run errands.

Kirsten suddenly felt the blood rushing from her face.

Errands? What kind of errands, at this hour, would a person run on Astor Place for his sister?

And the answer hit her—hard.

"Scott . . . ," Kirsten said, swallowing back her dry throat. "Who is your little sister . . . the one you're doing the errand for?"

"You wouldn't know her," Scott said. "Why?"

"Is her name . . . Gina?"

Scott stood up slowly. A smile spread across his face, and Kirsten knew the answer before he opened his mouth.

"You say the strangest things, Kirsten," he said. "I usually don't like to talk about my sister. That's one thing I reserve for myself. My personal life. That's one thing I don't like losing control over. See, to me, the most important thing is CONTROL."

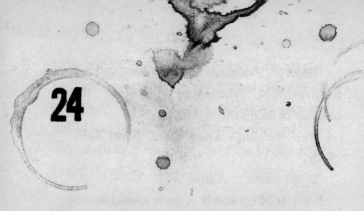

24

He was the one. Of course.

Scott. A killer.

He was the only one who knew them all.

He was there at the Zoo tending bar the night Kyle fought with Carolee, when he was Paul. The night he left his tie on the bar and stormed off . . . with his pals. Scott found the tie, held it in the lost-and-found for Kyle to retrieve. But then Scott got the news. The news that his sister had been killed. By a car full of boys. Boys who had driven off, leaving an innocent, bleeding ninth grader.

All except Kyle, who'd jumped out and stayed with her.

"He was the only one who'd tried to help her," Kirsten said, "who *cared* about her."

"Oh, he did?" Scott said, his face now icy cold. "Unfortunately, it doesn't fit with what I saw. I was there, Kirsten. When I heard what happened, I came running. *Do you know what it feels like to turn the corner and see someone running away from your dead sister?"*

"You saw him because he was the only one who stayed with her!" Kirsten shot back. "He held her when she was dying. When the other guys drove away."

"That's not what *they* told me."

"*Who* told you? Goldstein? Moyer? Those lowlife cokeheads? *They were lying!*"

Scott had backed her against the door to the next car. His breath came at her in warm, Scotch-scented bursts. "Willets . . . Schloss . . . all of them. Individually. The identical story. Your boyfriend was *driving*, Kirsten. He *aimed* at her. *'We just want to hold hands!'* That's what he said as he smashed into her. Can you imagine? He stayed with Gina *because they threw him out and drove to get help*! He felt her twitching and"—Scott's voice choked—"and he strangled her to death. Finished the job— probably so she wouldn't tell the cops!"

"That's not true," Kirsten said.

"I tend bar for all you condescending rich kids. . . . I clean your puke and give you advice, and I listen to your sob stories about the hard

life in ten-million-dollar apartments and look
the other way at your fake I.D.s and serve you
drinks and hold on to your blow, and I throw
out anyone who threatens your well-scrubbed,
immaculate asses and smile and say thank you
to your clueless cheap tips and *I protect you
from the idea that anything you do might be wrong
or illegal or God forbid unwise, because I am Scott
the stupid, low-class bartender—and I say*
SCREW YOU, KIRSTEN. SCREW YOU AND
ALL YOUR GODDAMN RICH UPPER
EAST SIDE OVERPRIVILEGED SCUMBAG
FRIENDS!" Scott reared back and swung.

"Ahhhhh!" Kirsten shrieked, ducking.

His fist connected with the metal wall so
hard, she swore she could feel the whole car
rock. "I'm sorry," he said, suddenly sounding
restrained and quiet. "That . . . was very bad.
That was a loss of *control.* Wouldn't you
agree?"

Kirsten nodded numbly. *He's about to kill
me,* she thought. *I am alone in a slow-moving
subway car, somewhere south of Eighty-sixth
Street, and by the time I reach Fifty-ninth, I will
be dead.*

"Put yourself in my shoes, Kirsten," Scott

said with a chilly calmness. "You're tending bar one night and you see a young guy, Paul, go crazy when he sees the love of his life screwing another guy—"

"That's not how it happened," Kirsten said. "Carolee wasn't—"

"Were you there? Or do you just *wish* you were there, waiting to get in his pants when he left the bar?" Scott cleared his throat. "Actually, you should have been there, throwing yourself at him. Then he would have been too busy to go out and kill Gina. And I wouldn't have had to . . . to . . ."

His face went slack, as if a cloud had passed across his eyes.

The train was speeding up now, just a bit.

"To get revenge?" Kirsten said, finishing his sentence. "To use his tie to kill Carolee? To frame him and ruin his future?"

"What . . . were . . . my . . . choices?" Scott asked, his voice a strangled whisper. "I loved my sister. She was smart, pretty, so beautiful. Unlike your parents, ours had no money, and I was going to put her through college. . . . *She was my life, Kirsten. He took MY LIFE! So what could I do? Kill him myself?* Have his blood on my hands and spend the rest of my life in jail? Gina wouldn't have wanted that. . . ."

"She wouldn't have wanted you to kill another innocent girl—"

"Carolee was not so innocent! You know who was innocent? *Gina* was innocent."

"And what about Sam? What did Sam do to deserve what she got?"

"Two years had gone by," Scott said. "I thought it was over. Your little boyfriend went to jail and was far, far away—and good riddance. Or so I thought. Then, two years later, he gets out and he has the balls to come back . . . to my bar . . . *and the asshole didn't even recognize me!"*

"So you needed to frame him again?" Kirsten cried. *"With Sam's life?"*

"He was supposed to rot in jail," Scott said through clenched teeth. "But his daddy got him out. What was I supposed to do—just sit by and watch this injustice?" he cried. "I was giving your boyfriend to the cops on a platter." Scott's voice grew distant. "But they were too stupid. They weren't going to find him, before he found me. So I decided to cut off the source. I did the thoughtful thing—"

"Killing him was *thoughtful?*"

"Because it spared the lives of others! After he was gone, I could stop." Scott said. The train's pace began to slacken. They would be at the station in a minute. "Or so I thought," he added, reaching underneath his jacket.

No. What is he doing? "Scott . . . ," Kirsten began, "maybe . . . maybe I can keep your secret. Maybe we can work something out."

"Sorry, kid. It's too late for that now," Scott said as he loosened his tie and pulled a knife from his belt.

25

"You can't!" Kirsten cried,

her mind racing. "You can't kill me here! There'll be people at the next stop! They'll see me. They'll see *you*!"

Scott brought the tip of the knife to her trembling jaw. "This . . . is . . . control. Like a surgeon. I can keep this a millimeter from you at will, for as long as I want, no matter how much you move. Want to try me?"

Kirsten gulped. She didn't dare nod.

"At the Fifty-ninth Street stop we will both walk out," he went on. "Calmly. Arm in arm. Like lovers. In fact, we can keep that option open because we will be heading west to Central Park."

He lowered his knife, hiding it in his overcoat, as the train slowed to a stop. The doors opened and they left, letting a tired-looking group of late-night stragglers file into the car behind them. A familiar mosaic sign on the wall said BLOOMINGDALE'S, advertising the famous department store, and Kirsten ached for the memory of her usual reason to stop here.

They turned a corner to the stairwell, and a voice called out, "Freeze!"

Russo!

"Shit," Scott muttered, grabbing Kirsten hard and pulling her back toward the tracks.

From one stairwell, Russo and two other cops swooped down; from the other, Peterson and another cop. They crouched, brandishing their guns. *"DON'T TRY ANYTHING STUPID!"* Russo shouted, over the screams of subway riders scurrying for the streets.

Scott's knife was out, and Kirsten could feel the presence of its tip like a baby's breath at her throat. "HE'S GOING TO KILL ME!" she cried out.

"Put the knife down," Russo said steadily.

"This is a little unbalanced, isn't it?" Scott answered back. "Put the guns down."

"It's over, Scott," Peterson said. "Last call. And you know it."

"Last call?" Scott nearly spat the words into the back of Kirsten's head. "It's not the last call. For any of us. My *sister* was the one who

had last call, pal. It was last call the day she was abandoned in the gutter by that rich-bastard boyfriend of *hers*."

Kirsten screamed, feeling the knife prick her skin.

"New York's *Finest*," Scott drawled sarcastically. "Where were you when Gina needed help? WHERE WERE YOU? Protecting the streets of area code 10021 for the investment bankers and brokers and swindlers who grease your palms enough so you can buy that Weber grill for your postage-stamp Massapequa backyard? *Last call for THAT, buddy!*" His hand was vibrating now.

The cops were silent, locked in position, and Kirsten's gaze darted from gun barrel to gun barrel.

They couldn't shoot. Could they? And if they didn't shoot, then what? Scott wasn't going to make it. The knife blade wasn't so steady anymore. She could feel the tip. The blood starting to trickle down her neck.

"S-S-Surgeon, remember?" Kirsten whispered. "C-C-Control?"

"Shut up." Scott pulled the blade lower and began stepping backward, toward the edge of the platform. "I am going to lower both of us to the tracks. We are going to walk into the tunnel, and then I am going to run. At which point, I release you and you're free—if you do as I say. *Do you understand me?*"

"Yes," Kirsten whispered back. Her chest was heaving with panicked breaths. She had to stay calm. If she did, there was a better chance that he would, too. He was being rational. Sparing her life. All she had to do was walk on the tracks

Be calm. Say yes. Don't blow it. Beneath her feet she felt the roughness of the yellow caution strip at the very edge of the platform. Scott was leading her to a small stairway at a lip near the end of the platform, where the MTA workers go down to the tracks.

But just then she felt a breeze on her skin. A shift of wind from the tunnel itself.

"A train," Scott said.

Kirsten heard the rumble coming from uptown. They couldn't go down on the tracks now.

Scott was frozen. Undecided.

And now, in the station, Richard Stone was racing down the stairs. Still dressed in rags. Still carrying a camera.

"Get back upstairs!" Peterson shouted.

At the sight of Richard, Scott began to shake. "Asshole . . . ," he murmured.

"Richard, get out of here!" Kirsten screamed.

But Richard was stunned. Just standing there, agape.

"Ignore him," Kirsten said. "Please."

"Get that asshole out of here!" Scott yelled.

Ca-chunk . . . ca-chunk . . . ca-chunk . . . Kirsten could hear the train approaching, by the noise on the rails. How far was it? Ten blocks? Ten yards?

Scott looked back to the track. Out to the station.

Peterson shifted his gun, ever so slightly.

Richard lifted his camera.

CA-CHUNK . . . CA-CHUNK . . . CA-CHUNK . . .

Closer. Much closer. Already creating a wind, pushing the air out of the tunnel.

"They don't listen!" Scott bellowed in her ear. "NOBODY LISTENS!" With a sudden grunt, he threw Kirsten backward.

And she tumbled . . . tumbled down, onto the tracks!

26

She hit the bottom hard.

Something snapped beneath her as she splashed into a foul-smelling puddle of unknown origins.

Dead. I'm dead.

CRACK!

A pistol shot rang out from above, and she flinched. Ahead, she saw two bright eyes. The lights of the train. Coming closer.

Kirsten screamed as a rat the size of a Volkswagen Beetle scurried across her hand and into a hole in the far wall off the tracks to safety.

Go! Get up! She scrambled to her feet. "Yeeeooooow!" she cried out in pain. Her ankle was shattered. She couldn't stand.

WONNNK! WONNNNNNK!

The train's blast was deafening. The brakes screeched.

The conductor had seen her.

He was three blocks away. Maybe two.

It can't end this way.

I can't die here!

GO!

Gritting her teeth, she reached up—to the pipes that ran along the edge of the platform, pulling herself with all her strength. Dragging her body.

WONNNNNNK!

The lights . . . like two eyes . . . widening . . . angry . . .

Could she tuck her body under . . . was there room under the platform? No. She would be sliced in half.

Scott's face, twisted into a wild grin, appeared over the edge of the platform. "Last . . . call," he said in a raspy voice.

"You can't," she said. *"Scott, help me! Help me up!"*

He continued to grin.

Move. Just move. She tried to haul herself toward the end of the platform. Near the stairs. There was an indentation there. Enough space for a human body.

But it was far. Too far.

And then she saw the hand. Reaching down toward her.

The hand covered with rivulets of blood.

Scott's hand.

"Grab it," he said.

No. He's going to kill you.

"Just grab it, Goddamn it!" Scott lunged farther over the edge and closed his thick fingers around her wrist. Kirsten screamed and struggled to shake lose, but she was rising . . . rising . . .

WONNNNNNK!

SSKKKREEEEEEEE!

The sound of the brakes was so loud, so near, so piercing, as if the train had become a part of her body. But she was out. Rolling onto the platform, crying out at the knife-edge pain in her ankle. Saved by Scott.

She looked toward him, but he was sprawled in a pool of blood. She saw the bullet entrance wound just below his right shoulder.

He looked at her with an expression she couldn't read. "I . . . loved her," he rasped, pushing himself along the platform with his legs . . . toward the track . . .

The front of the train was charging into

the station now, along with the smell of burning metal. And Kirsten realized what he was trying to do. "No, Scott!" she cried out. "Don't!"

"Last call," Scott repeated. With one mighty gesture, he grabbed the edge of the platform and hauled himself over.

Kirsten turned her head away as the Number 5 screamed in.

EPILOGUE

Kirsten set her crutches near the bar. It had been six weeks since she'd gone out at night. Six weeks since she broke her ankle in a dozen places. Six weeks of excruciating pain. Of constant physical therapy.

And relief. Incredible, blessed relief.

The murders were over. Truly over.

Kirsten's gala Spring Coming Out Party was Julie's idea, of course.

It was late March—almost spring break—the weather was finally starting to thaw, and Kirsten was feeling human for the first time in ages.

"Piña coladas all around!" Julie announced. "Today, our beloved former Woodley Queen comes back to the real world—*and is she ready to par-tyyyyy!*"

"WOOOOO!" shouted Carla, and the entire crowd—everyone who was anyone—at Rampage, the latest and greatest club on the

Upper East Side. Carla raised a glass and started dancing to some new hip-hop song.

Kirsten had picked out the track. She couldn't dance yet, but she'd sure had plenty of time to watch MTV while lying flat on her back. She glanced around at the raging new place, bopping her head in time with the bass. No, it wasn't the Party Room. Nothing would be like the Party Room, but the three *amigas* had decided that they just couldn't go there anymore—too many bad memories. And besides, the Party Room was *so* high school. It was time for a new haunt.

She smiled at the motion, the lights on the dance floor, the scent of sex, alcohol, and teen spirit. It felt good. Really good.

All winter in the hospital and at home, Kirsten hadn't been able to move. Through her bedroom window she stared at the snow settling on the bare canopies of Central Park's trees, the school groups bouncing up and down the steps of the Metropolitan Museum, the gliding of redwing hawks over the Reservoir. She'd eaten Häagen-Dazs ice cream, watched TV, read, took house calls from her shrink, attempted catching up on her schoolwork, Web-surfed, IM'ed. Diligently. Furiously. Trying to forget.

Sleep had been rare and awful, the memories haunting her in the dark. Sam and Emma and Kyle . . . the thick streak of blood leading to the edge of the subway platform, ending at the silver bottom of the Number 5 train whose conductor had tried so hard to stop in time . . . the thick shoulders of Russo and Peterson, who attempted to comfort her as squadrons of police descended into the Fifty-ninth Street–Bloomingdale's station she vowed to never again visit . . . the heavy, creaky clanking of the train as it was backed up slowly, back over Scott's body in order to retrieve it. . . .

At times, it seemed the spring would never come and she would be bedridden forever. Tonight felt as if she'd died and gone to heaven.

"And," Sarah announced, waving her arm to the crowd in a *very* unstable way, "to celebrate her freedom and her return to the world of—"

"Sex," Julie added.

"And just in time for spring break," Sarah said, pulling out a stack of boxes from underneath a table, "we have chipped in for a new wardrobe!"

"Oh. My. God," Kirsten said as Julie pulled out a teeny black LaPerla bra-and-panty set, an orange Yves Saint Laurent bikini, a push-up bra with Janet Jackson star cut-outs, and a pair of stiletto beach shoes.

"Yyyyyes!" shouted Brandon Yardley, his arm around the senator's daughter whose name Kirsten couldn't remember but who smacked him so hard on the cheek that he nearly fell over.

Kirsten held each item, spreading them over her funky little Betsy Johnson dress and groaning with dismay. "I. Am. So. *FAAAAT!*"

"We thought of that, too," Julie said.

"Huh?" Kirsten replied.

"So we bought you, just in time for Bermuda beach season, three weeks of daily physical therapy with . . . Gay Gabe!"

And there he was, the guy once voted Woodley's Hottest Butt four years in a row, now a physical trainer at Crunch and wearing, well, just enough to cover what was necessary.

Sort of.

"How may I . . . serve you?" Gabe said, wiggling his way across the floor to a roar of laughter.

"Cruel," Kirsten said, burying her face in her hands. "So cruel."

In a moment, Gabe was off dancing with Carla and Sarah, the place was bouncing, and Julie was shoving another drink into Kirsten's hand. "Happy?"

"Yeah," Kirsten said.

"Still thinking about . . . you know?"

Kirsten shrugged. "There was good news today. Peterson called me before I came here—it comes out in the *Times* tomorrow. Kyle's name was officially cleared in the murders of Carolee, Sam, Emma . . . *and* Gina. They found hard evidence to nail Scott on the first three murders—and for Lauren's. And, by the way, a cut on his scalp matched the edge of the toilet paper dispenser I smacked him with at Yellow Trance. They're pretty confident they're going to bring in Goldstein and that gang on Gina's killing, too."

"The important thing is," Julie said gently, "does it give you some closure?"

Kirsten winced. She didn't like that word. "I guess. But it's never really over. . . ." She turned her head toward the bar and shouted,

"Especially if Rich decides to make that damn movie!"

"If he can get his film back from the damn police!" came a loud answer.

Richard Stone was standing behind the bar with his thumb on the blender, making what must have been his thousandth piña colada of the night. He wasn't allowed back at NYU until next semester—until the police and the campus administration gave him the okay. In the meantime, this job would tide him over.

"Anyway, with all my tip money I'm developing a different kind of project," Richard said. "A departure from the Richard Stone oeuvre. A location shoot. I think I'll call it *Woodley Bitches Do Bermuda.* What do you think? With a hip-hop score and a couple of over-the-top twists, it could be The Next Big Thing!"

"Do you know what he's talking about?" Julie asked.

"Well, it sounds like this movie is going to require a *lot* of tips," Kirsten said.

WHHIIIIIR . . . went the blender.

"Piña coladas all around!" Richard shouted.

Kirsten looked at Julie. Julie looked at

Kirsten. They both burst out laughing.

"I think this will be the best spring ever," Julie said.

"It's about time," Kirsten said. She reached into her bag and gave Julie a wad of bills to drop into Richard's tip jar. Who knew? Maybe he really was the next Tarantino. Maybe not.

For the time being, he was a hell of a good bartender.

And that was just fine.

A house at the beach.
A bunch of hot strangers.
A three-month party that's
off the hook.

Catch the first two books in a hot new series from Simon Pulse.

summer

share

CC

Cape Cod

LB

Laguna Beach

by Randi Reisfeld

by Nola Thacker

6 STRANGERS.
1 CRASH PAD.
ENDLESS PARTIES . . .

SHARE THE LOVE!

Britney is the girl everyone
loves to hate.

She's popular, blond, and fabulous.
Sure, people are jealous. . . .

But jealous enough to want her dead?

killing britney

A thrilling new novel by Sean Olin
from Simon Pulse • published by Simon & Schuster

Feel the Fear.

FEAR STREET® NIGHTS

A brand-new Fear Street trilogy by the master of horror

R.L. STINE

In Stores Now

Simon Pulse
Published by Simon & Schuster
FEAR STREET is a registered trademark of Parachute Press, Inc.